Serpents in the Garden
A Thunder of Dragons

By Randy A. Cook

Published by eGenesis Media

Serpents in the Garden

Copyright

Published in the United States by
eGenesis Media
23097 Wallace Road
Parsons, KS 67357
Visit our website at www.eGenesisMedia.com

ISBN: 978-0-9894646-1-1

Dedication

For all the people in my life who have in some way helped to hold my own darker Dragons at bay for yet another day. Larry, Vicky, Regina, Ray, Greg, Stephanie, Dale, and especially Spencer to name a few.

Serpents in the Garden

Table of Contents

Children of Tiamate
By Randy A. Cook

Creation
Children of Tiamate
Prolog

Tiamate. The Void. No light or its absence, the dark. Such things had not yet come into existence since existence itself had yet to be realized. Tiamate, the Great Dragon, whose coils wrap around all that might someday be. Sleeping... Dreaming... Waiting...

Then there was something else, something different. Something not of the Void, an irritating speck in the eye of the unseen worm. Tiamate stirred in what should have been his eternal slumber in response to this presence that he did not recognize or understand.

For so long, forever, he had been alone and now to be... not alone. The Dragon opened wide his eyes to see this foreign something. To gaze at what now stood before him in all of its oddness, its disgusting separateness.

However, the alien presence did not want to be known, did not even fully recognize that the Void watched him in wonder. He only knew himself and called his own name, Marduke. He had much work ahead of him, or perhaps behind him, he did not know or care. The arrow of time had not yet been given flight and that was the first of his many tasks.

Tiamate watched as the presence pulled forth a sword forged of something else as well. Again, this difference that was not of himself. Raising the sword high over his head, with both hands on the hilt, this creature called Marduke prepared. The Dragon looked on not understanding, not comprehending what this tiny little thing was doing.

With one strong downward motion, Marduke cleaved the Void. Tiamate recoiled as the blade cut deep into his being. He did not know what pain was, even as he felt it burn through his oneness. Pain was as unfamiliar as this speck that caused it. Again, the sword was raised and fell and the Void was split in two.

Marduke watched as half fell to his feet and was made solid, and the other was cast into what was to become the sky. Suddenly there was light and dark as the world took sinister form and shape, and the heavens lit up casting radiance upon this new creation.

Marduke looked into his own reflection held in the endless blackness like a mirror and struck the mirror with the hilt of his sword. His image was shattered and the broken shards stepped into this new existence and stood beside him. His brothers, his sisters in creation.

Nevertheless, the heavens retched at the violence of the forced division of the Void and rained down upon the earth in fiery retribution of the separation of the two seeking reunion as it was before. A return to the oneness.

Thus was shot the arrow of time and the war of creation begun. For Tiamate neither wanted or would allow for this blaspheme to continue; and the clan of Marduke would not permit it to be stopped The many drops of the Dragon's blood that fell to the world, these Children of Tiamate, would take back that which was stolen and end the pain of the world caused by the fractured Gods of men.

aZaTHaRaK
Draco Terra
Children of Tiamate
Part I

The earth moved as if it were liquid, radiating a dark red heat that permeated all. Rock became water and water became steam. Waves of granite and lead pressed firm against the confining crust of the upper world, where a rock is as hard as a rock, and water is a raindrop. Deep within the bowels of the planet that was his prison, the dragon aZaTHaRaK stirred from a millennium long slumber. Massive wings pressed hard against molten rock and the dragon began to swim outward, towards the surface. A swirling collage of blacks and golds followed each beat of the wings. And the surface began to tremble at his approach, for it feared his presence.

The first of the tremors were small, dislodging only tiny pebbles. The second was larger, causing the trees to shudder. The third ripped the trees asunder and reduced the mightiest of the nearby stones to dust. The earth belched up clouds of steam, and a vomit of lava flowed across the shrubs and grasses, turning them to ash. A shape began to move amongst the smoke and stench. The form rose up on wings of chaos and filled the air, casting down to the earth a blackened shadow of coming death.

Some distance away, far removed from the stirrings of the earth, unaware that what was once held below the surface was rising up, he watched her. A young man in his prime searched her out without ever actually reaching out. Standing in the shadows, he watched; he waited almost afraid of what he was waiting for. A look? A smile? A touch perhaps? An opportunity? A stirring within that he both hated and yearned for. But, desire overwhelmed self-loathing, so he continued to wait and watch.

In the calm and quiet of a forest clearing, the young woman laid upon a bed of grass green. Flowers of pale pinks and light blues were woven with intricate care through her locks of long golden hair. In a gown of soft satin and delicate lace, she slept, never feeling the movement of the earth, or seeing the shadow that grew about her, a shadow that blackened the clearing as if it were night. A danger so near and yet unrecognized.

It was not until the hot wind of his breath circled about her, that she awoke to look into his cold ebony eyes.

But she alone did not watch the scaled shape of the beast, for the young man was near held captive by his ache and he too felt the earth tremble as he watched her gasp at the coming dragon. They both saw as the creature rose from the depths of its earthen sea and advanced seeking its own opportunity. Foolish youth gave courage prompting a man to be fancied a knight. Placing helmet on head, and drawing sword from sheath, the knight prepared for battle. The edge of his blade glistened in the sunlight, from point to hilt it glowed with a brilliant radiance of self importance. He pushed into the valley, his weapon a mirror of the sun. To defend the maiden in lace from this abomination of love was his mission and his crusade. He wanted her love, and he wanted his fame. Moreover, in this heroic act, this rebellion against his own darker nature, he might win both.

"Hold spawn of Shaitan," the knight commanded, "turn and face the sword of a man."

Eyes of black on black turned and stared at the youthful warrior, whose own eyes shined of the blue sky. A single second became a thousand years, as old eyes fixed on the new. The air was hot, but the eyes were cold, and the mortal man shivered as he saw the patterns of a multitude of untold ancient stars reflected in the cold blackness contained in the beast's twin orbs. He saw, in likeness, the light from his own soul, a mere flickering flame in a vast sea of night. His hot youthful fire and the dragon's ancient cold flame, so very similar, and yet he would weakly deny this bold claim and point to differences of mere surfaces and textures while ignoring the burning meat of the matter . His will was not this lustful vice, his fire not drowning in the same.

Scaled flesh drew back from the corners of the serpent's mouth, and from far behind the multitude of teeth, words came forth. The voice was a long, low rumble of thunder and a hot gale of wind followed it. The dragon spoke: "I am aZaTHaRaK... eldest son of the Sixth Star... on the Northern Hemisphere... of the Third Strike." The creature flexed long talons of granite grey bone and sucked breath unto its mouth to continue. "Born in heaven and buried in earth, above and below will be returned as before, I claim what is mine by right."

Man-made armour of tempered steel forged by fire and hammer can protect this mortal from the mightiest of blows; but it is not with mere physical forces that the dragon attacks. The human mind is not prepared to encompass the infinite depth of the inferno's chasm. When exposed to the endless depths of the void, the mortal mind is paralyzed, and a heavy scaled hand laid him low to the ground. The ebony eyes, once again, turned towards the virgin maid.

It matters not if she be a true virgin to man, for all things are virgin to the beast.

An icy grip and burning whispers answered the ranting and rage of the virgin maid. Screams froze the moment, and time sent the sound to the boundaries of the forest and beyond. The world could not breathe for the grip was near too tight, and if a single gasp were possible, the air would reek of a choking death.

"Nay, I say unto ye dragon!" aZaTHaRaK heard the words and felt the blade that followed.

Cutting deep into the leathery hide of the dragon, the young knight shouted, "Mortal hands did fashion armour to protect my body, but it is a divine hand that protects my soul. I would be knight and I will be worthy of that honor. God is my witness; I will resist that which I must."

The dragon rose up and slashed with talon and teeth. The noble knight, or so he desperately desired to be, parried iron to talon, but had nothing to offer the teeth, save for his flesh and bone. Blood flowed in an ever-expanding stain on the youth's tunic. Armour was pierced as easily as flesh, and the dragon's ivory daggers were red with blood. The sword grew heavy as the warrior's strength threatened to flow through the wounds, but the arm refused to give in to the weakness and continued to drive the blade with a fierce determination.

Like stone against stone, each thrust of his sword gave birth to a moment of sparks. Just as granite gives little care to the strike of a chisel, the dragon seemed not to notice the thrust of the blade. But, each of the dragon's blows brought deadly wounds and painful reminders to the knight that he could not lose this battle. Too much was at stake: his very humanity, his morality and his mortality.

Pain glazed his eyes and darkness threatened to push his thoughts from the light of consciousness, but it was fear that held the night at bay and faith that lit the blackening corners of his mind. To give into the darkness would be an easy escape, a cool darkness that hid a rainbow promising an eternity of rest. A multitude of vivid colours to entice the eye and relax the mind. But when revealed, it is nothing more than mist in the sky, given brilliance by the sun. The struggle to survive with honor intact has never been easy. He held his sword firm, its point centered on the attacking beast. The creature moved side-to-side waiting for the moment of greatest weakness that would offer him the throat of the youth.

The earth began to bubble and steam filled the air. What pain refused to hide, the smoke would try. In a mist of concealment, the dragon staked its prey. But the prey refused to be blinded; he knew the dragon was out there… watching, waiting.

"My light may be fading, and my body broken, but a greater power than they, do I pray to know and call," the words were defiant shouts of the knight's last inner reserves. With strength no longer his own, he cast his sword into the swirling clouds evoked by the monster. The weapon was no longer in mortal hands. Through gaps in the misty air, the sun brightly shined, and once again, the light reflected against the sword's now gleaming surface. It would be through illumination that the warrior would prevail.

A moment passed, followed by a minute. The young knight expected the dragon's heated breath to bear down upon him and a clawed hand to end his life.

Next came a cool breeze clearing the mist, the sound of a woman crying softly drifted through the air. The knight stood and watched the form of the slain dragon sink into the earth, his sword buried deep in its flesh, the molten prison of the planet's core taking back it prisoner. He walked to the woman who knelt on the field. She took hold of his hand and her tears washed clean the blood and the soiled remains of his mortal sins.

eLeVeeTHeN
Serpens Oceani
Children of Tiamate
Part II

The waves rolled out onto the land that was the shore, faltered, then retreated back into the endless desert of the sea. Moments later, the waves, the same and yet different, returned with greater force to lay claim to a tiny bit more of the sandy beach, before withdrawing again. The Lady Eliza would walk these shores, at this late hour, and watch the flow and ebb of the tide. The eternal battle between land and its neighbor the sea. She stared out across the watery void and waited for something, but was never quite sure for what she waited. The obvious is sometimes never as clear as one might expect.

High above her on the rocky cliff that overlooked the blue-green desert stood the castle of her husband. This stone fortress was generations old, and had served her Lord's family well for many centuries. Still, the castle guarded the shoreline, but the only battle that ever raged, was between the wet sea and the dry sand.

"Times be changing," she remembered the voice of her husband, "peasants revolt and land is lost. The noble class must find new ways to maintain and sustain itself." She reflected on these words and wondered at what he was doing so very far from home, from his familiar shores.

He used such strange words as "invest," and "diversify," and "I'll return in a matter of days."

It was over land that he left, and it would be by land that he returned. That in itself seemed odd to her. For it was always the sea that held the Lady Eliza's attention. The endless and eternal sea. As a child, she would stare out into the water blue for hours, lost in a dream world of dolphins and ancient turtles. On this dark night, the sea was a black and silver mirror, reflecting the multitude of stars that held sway over the heavens. A looking glass that held the universe in its shimmering surface.

She held the hem of her skirt up, and away from the sand and moisture of the beach. Her toes however, wiggled in the moving surge. The water that splashed against her feet was warm, as she waded out into the coming tide. Her destination was a small outcrop of rocks that formed an island when the tide was full.

The rocks were jagged, and it required great care to find a suitable place to recline. But the Lady Eliza was determined, and practiced, and at long last, she found her perfect perch and took rest, her back against the cool stone. The moon hung heavy in the sky, and so too did her eyes.

Lazily, she dragged her toes through the rising water, casting ripples out in an ever-widening ring, until they were consumed by larger ripples that became waves. She raised her foot high into the air and watched the water drip from her heel.

Although her foot no longer stirred the water, the water continued to be stirred, and bubbles rose from the shallow currents. With a child's fascination, the Lady Eliza looked into this swirling water and into her own reflection. Her image began to waiver, as the agitation in the water increased. The spinning and swirling of the water formed a whirlpool beside her tiny temporary island. The water began to move so fast that all the light from the reflected stars and her own image merged into a twinkling dance on the water's surface.

"What is this?" she asked aloud, questioning this strange occurrence. No answer was expected, but at her words, the whirlpool leaped into the air, dragging with it a jet of water. The cyclone swelled in size and increased in its frenzy. The moving wall of water engulfed the tiny island and threatened to tear it from the earth and set it adrift in the open sea.

She gave only a small startled gasp, as the water drenched her. She was not yet convinced it was real: a childhood dream perhaps, or a ride on the mare of the night. But nay to these, for from crown to toe she was wet. The wind whipped up and around her; she was blinded by the gale, the sea, and her own unveiled hair.

A terror at long last took hold, a scream caught in her throat that was trying to tear its way from her mouth. But the scream was still born, for the wind went silent and the water died down. In that split of an instant, it was over. The long curls of her damp auburn hair, did she lift from her eyes so as to see again.

The colour of sea green and aqua blue moved before her. She drew back her gaze and saw that the colour had a form, and it was a form unlike any she had ever seen before.

Scales of aquamarine covered a body, serpentine in shape. Wings of virescent fins flexed in the near dark of the moon, as wet drops of the salty sea caught the stray moonlight and glistened in reflection.

The Lady Eliza closed her eyes least she faint dead away. And in the darkness of her mind, the Dragon spoke. The voice was far away and distant, as if spoken from across the sea, a long wash from a secluded depth. She strained to hear the words, "I know thee sea child, and now thou shall know me. I be eLeVeeTHeN... third born of the twin suns... first to fall... of the second strike."

"What doest thou wish of me Serpent?" her words were whispers carried on trembling lips.

"Born in the sky, cast into the sea, these all shall be made one through thee. I take what be mine by right," the distant voice said.

The Lady Eliza felt the cool moistness of the Dragon's touch, and felt his icy breath on her neck. She feared from him, her pain, and knew that fight was in vain. The many tears she shed were lost to the sea. Salt to salt.

And once done was the deed, she was given the serpent seed, and down into the depths sank the Dragon of the sea.

As she rose from the rocks, the tide had drained away leaving an island no longer. Questing for the beach, the distant voice reached her, "I shall return unto thee one day."

Walking up the path towards the castle top, the Lady Eliza paused, and glanced back at the waiting sea. "My husband should return by land, not from thee," she spoke to the waters now calm.

The next night she walked out on the soft sand, and then returned to her bed in the castle high, far and lonely from the water's edge.

On the third night, she ventured into the splash of the tide, but only to her ankles did she wash.

On the forth, she returned to the tidal island and waited in the dark. Long into the night, the waters stirred and the Dragon rose. From his blue green father, he returned to her, and she embraced him, as he did embrace her.

Many days did pass, and many a night as well. It was on a dusk such as this that the Lord of the castle keep did return.

He made his way along the beach; wife and castle were his goal. He spied his wife walking along the water's edge, and stopped to watch her beauty, while she was yet unaware. With such grace did she move, her auburn hair flowing in the gentle wind. She stopped, the water lapping at her small feet, and he watched his beloved staring out at the sea.

The water churned beside her, the Lord wondered at this event. The Lady seemed not to notice, as the ocean spewed up a demon sent. The Dragon stood beside her, the Lord feared for his wife. She slowly turned and kissed it. The Lord unsheathed his sword and knife.

16

A mighty rage did possess the man and he screamed a bloody oath. He cursed the Serpent lover who embraced his beautiful betrothed.

Sword hit scale and tooth hit mail. Iron tempered with fire slashed and flashed against the coral hard shell of a Dragon's tail. He hit for the eye, he was going to make the Dragon die. He cut at the throat; he wanted its water born carcass to bloat. The battle shook the sand and blood mixed with the sea.

The Lady Eliza pleaded in desperation; she begged them to stop. Her voice went unheard, so to her knees she did drop. The bloody water stained more than her dress as she waited to see who would come out best.

With a powerful scream, the sword pierced the Dragon's heart. The Serpent form withered, and then lay still, sinking slowly beneath the waves. Tiamate takes back its own.

The bloody and bruised Lord of the seaside castle did rise up from the battle scene. With slow and pained steps, he made his way to his lady dear. However, she did not see him, for she was staring out across the watery void, waiting for something, and now, she knew for what she waited… her beloved, the Serpent of the sea.

yTyPHyMyS
Ignis Vermis
Children of Tiamate
Part III

Mountains of grey granite and trees of evergreen beckoned to the bright and shining daystar. Slowly, but without hesitation, the sun fell into the embrace of the earth, thus, at dusk, the Lady Eleanor began her journey. She kissed her Lord Husband goodbye and he bid her a safe journey.

The day before, she had told him that she would visit her ailing mother yet again. Once, sometimes twice a month, she would journey away from her husband's estates to see to the care of her failing mother.

Her husband often insisted that he should accompany her, but she always declined saying, "mother is a proud woman, and does not wish for you to see her in this pitiful state."

Her husband, a proud man himself, accepted this with regret. And so he watched her travel through the castle gates. He would listen to the sound of the carriage wheels clicking against the cobblestone as she rolled away, and then to the silence that remained after she was gone.

The journey was not long, seven maybe eight hours at the most. The Lady Eleanor would stare out into the dark countryside framed by the carriage window with its drapes of purples and reds, and think her silent thoughts that were never shared with her husband or mother. Looking at the pale lights flickering from the windows of the huts and shacks that they pasted, she would cover her mouth and nostrils to prevent the stench of the inhabitants and their wretched lives from offending her senses. She turned from the window and the peasants that she knew were far too close, and looked down at the jeweled rings on her hands and reach to her breast and stroked the golden broach as it set at its proper place. These were just trinkets compared to what she would someday posses once her foolish husband and ill mother were... dismissed. The Lady Eleanor set her gaze forward and sat in silence. Choosing instead to focus her inner attention on the things to come, and the anticipation she so dearly loved. She reflected on these private things and her hands began to sweat as they always did at this time.

To her impatience, the hours passed and the entrance of her mother's lands finally came into view.

The driver slowed the horses and brought them to halt at the gate, as he had done so many times before. The house was yet a quarter of a mile beyond this point, but he knew his mistress' preferences. She always insisted on walking the winding lane. To argue the point had constantly proven useless in the past, and he no longer even tried for fear of the repercussions.

The Lady Eleanor was born on this land and favored to stroll the lane at this late hour, as she had done when she was young.

After helping the Lady Eleanor from her soft cushions, the driver turned the carriage and began the trip home. He had been told that the visit would last five days, and he would return then to retrieve his Mistress.

The Lady Eleanor watched the carriage depart and looked down the lane that lay before her. The stones were like familiar friends, for she knew each stride of the path well, but it was a path she would not yet travel, and they were friends she would not disturb with her steps. Turning away from the lane that led to the house, she chose instead to walk further down the darkened road.

The moon hung heavy in the sky and a million stars shone down upon her. Nothing disturbed her footfalls, and when a carriage happened to approach, she would hide in the forest's edge until it had passed, then she would continue her dark shrouded movements.

At a point guided by a second nature born of a lifetime of habit, more so than the light of the moon as it shined through the tree tops casting long and foreboding shapes with its half creatures that belonged more to the imagination than here in the real world, she strayed from the path of God fearing men and women and entered deep into the forest.

Now, far and removed from the eyes of most men, she reached a small meadow. From the edge of the clearing, she gathered wood, leaves, and dried shrubs.

Placing them in a pile at the center of the clearing, she began the process of making a fire. The twigs and leaves quickly caught the spark she created. Tree limbs and logs she dragged into the fire to feed its heat.

High into the night the flames reached. The wind swayed the blaze, and it danced, back and forth to an unheard beat of an ancient song. On the earth around the blazing promenade, the Lady Eleanor etched strange signs and symbols. These were enclosed by a double lined circle, and at each point of the compass, she scribed words unpronounceable to the Christian mouth.

Once done, she stopped all movement, and every sound became silence, for the forest went strangely quiet. No bird or cricket dared to interrupt the stillness. Nor did the games keeper speak as he hid in the dark shadow of a great oak. Fear and fascination held him froze to his spying pose. The poachers hunting this night had gained a moment's reprieve from the landlord's justice.

Then the Lady Eleanor gave birth to the unheard song, and the blaze responded with an intensity of reds, yellows and oranges. Her voice rose and fell in a distorted hymn, and sweat beaded on her brow. The forest knew fear, but the fire felt passion, and a shape began to move within the heat and smoke.

Her song stopped, and she waited. A smile formed on her lips, even as they continued to mouth the unspoken words of making. Her eyes searched the flames for a familiar shape.

The colour of gold formed on the fire's edge, at the boundary between a realm possessed of light, heat and burning cold, in constant motion and resistance, touching against the world as known by man, a real thing of substance unaffected by that, which is not of this world's nature, or of the nature of God. The edge of the world's pain and the great inferno; the golden door opens. And beyond that portal, a great shadow stirred. A massive form moved forward and advanced upon the earth.

From the heart of the fire, stepped a creature who mocked the form of a man. Strong arms flexed and stretched in the hot rising air, and a handsome face beamed from underneath locks of golden blonde curls that flowed gently in the spiraling up draft. Powerful legs supported a trunk that rippled with muscular vitality. And that which made him a man would truly have been any man's pride, for he was every woman's dream of a comely man. But he was not a mortal, for wings of fire extended from his back, and a glowing halo of heated light spouted as a crown from his head. His eyes were blacker than the night that surrounded the clearing, and yet they held a fire of their own. To the Lady Eleanor he was a god. Words sang from his lips, and an invisible choir joined in to make his voice a symphony, "I be yTyPHyMyS, twelfth born of the sixty sixth child of the Great Void. Dawned in the northern Lights, condemned to the waning embers. The light and dark seek to abandon their forced nature and once again become one. I take what be mine by rights."

The mighty arms of the one spawned by fire reached out to the Lady Eleanor, and she fell into his grasp. His touch was cold against her fire-heated skin, even as he moved within her; she could feel the frost from his breath. Pain merged with ecstasy and consciousness faded from the Lady Eleanor's mind.

The next morn, she awoke on the ground. Gone was her lover, but she was not alone. The fire was spent, and only charred ashes remained. Her freedom, like the smoke had also vanished. The cleric, that lorded over her, and his heavy-handed retainers were seeing to that. She was allowed to collect her cloths, and once presentable, they headed for the road, and her eventual trial.

The eyes of a common grounds keeper had seen her, and his words had convicted her. A woodsman looking for poachers had caught a witch.

In a torch lit chamber, hidden within the bowels of the fortress like cathedral of Saint Marcus the Defender, the high inquisitor of the counsel of Vindication presided over her trial. A scourge of heretics. A burner of witches. This was how the priest was known. His name was unimportant, and forgotten by most, only his mission resides in the minds of those who attended the inquiry.

The pleas of the accused's husband were heard and held in suspicion, for he was of either a great evil himself in league with the witch and her demon familiar, or still a greater fool for not seeing the Dragon for what it was.

Justice was quick and from her darkened cell, the Lady Eleanor could still hear the final words:

"Having been convinced of your sins by irrefutable testimony in this court and in the presence of the All Mighty God, this tribunal has no choice but to find you guilty of the crime of witchcraft, a treasonous act against the Church, State, and God. To save your soul and purge the evil demons of your oppression, we sentence you to be burned at the stake. Confine her until the appointed time of her salvation."

The woman did not resist, fight, or cry; Eleanor could see no point in losing what was left of her dignity by begging for mercy. Man's mercy was not a quality reserved for witches, and God's mercy is apparently subject to earthly interpretation. She looked around the court into the eyes of all those good God fearing Christians and began to laugh. It was not a weak laugh, or a nervous laugh, but a full-bodied voice that mocked the court. So upright they were. So full of self-satisfying superiority. In the name of God, they think to throw me out, as if they were worthy to interpret the will of God. How convenient that God's will so often mirrored their own decadent desires. Her chuckles continued to echo through the courtroom long after the hooded instrument of God's mercy on earth removed her.

The fallen lady was not concerned by the verdict of the court, the influence of earthly matters have no lasting impression on the immortal soul; she drew comfort knowing that her lover was a creature of the fire and he would greet her in that funeral pyre as her savior, even as the flames liberated her spirit of this material plane of existence.

And at the appointed time, she was taken to the mound of ash upon which a pile of timber had been stacked. This hallowed acre of earth had heard the many screams of a multitude of witches. She was lashed to the stake at the center of the mound, high above all others on her podium of brittle dry wood. The priests performed their rituals and the fire was set. Familiar flames sprang up around her and filled her vision. She sang her words of Making, until the smoke choked off her voice, but she knew no fear, for her god was with her.

The pain and heat were felt for only a moment. The mind shuts down what it cannot take and she was left in the darkness of her own mind. Then she heard it, the choir that was the voice of her lover.

In the darkness of her death, she looked about, grasping for a glance of the eternal light of her love. The cool embrace of his powerful arms. In the distance, on this flat plane of the void, she saw the glint of his light, the halo of his approach. The golden door once again opened, and the shadows of the other side moved forward to find her waiting.

But that which stepped forth from the shimmering portal was not the form of her expectations, for her master no longer assumed the shape of a man. The Great Dragon of the flames walked the earth in all of his hideous glory. And the majestic orchestra of his voice repeated the words that Eleanor knew so well:

"I be yTyPHyMyS, and I take what be mine by rights."

A massive back draft from the Dragon's breath pulled Eleanor towards him and his golden door. And where once fear could not find a home, it now found an eternal residence. And the flames that the mortal mind refused to acknowledge, the soul could not deter.

The tears shed will never extinguish the pyro for greed and want of power will always be consumed and left as ash.

stAkArAl
Spiritus Draconis
Children of Tiamate
Part IV

The angel stAkArAl flew towards the Earth, the Garden, a faux Eden created not in the wake of God, but in his absence. He carried with him the words of a missing God. Glowing orbs of unnatural essence that were so very much a part of the natural order. No one except the intended would even recognize much less hear and understand that which was contained in these spheres. Each orb was a blessed syllable that spoke an infinite volume to be whispered into the ear of humanity, and it was stAkArAl, who was charged with delivering these whispers.

Light shown round about him, separating him from the darkness as he moved forward on shimmering wings that parted the cold of space from the vast heat of the world. He knew nothing of light, or dark, or of cold and heat, he simply was as he was intended to be, both intimate with all, and oblivious to everything. Everything, save that which he was tasked to do. He made his way towards Earth, to mankind, bearing these gifts, this was his greatest and most honored of duties.

The shadows that encircled the world could see the shine of his approach and moved in their own purpose to intercept. A purpose not spoken of in the halls of heaven, but held in the hearts of certain men and the dark primeval urges that they served. They wanted the bright spheres for themselves.

The darkness of space and bitter heart moved with violence against the Angel. Although the seraph, who held no light of his own, but rather reflected the light of his maker, was constructed of mighty things, he was not all-powerful, and even more mightier things were sent against him. One ensnared his right hand and held it firm, while another stabbed cold carbon at his chest. Twisted tentacles wrapped around his legs and sought to pull him from the blue skies.

The darkness spread its own foul wings and blotted out the sun.

stAkArAl struggled, but lost his grip on the orbs, and one fell to the earth so very far below. He cried out and a Host was with him. The sky was a fire with light and brilliance as if heaven itself had opened up and the very stars seemed dimmed and shaded in comparison. The darkness retreated.

stAkArAl plunged towards the earth as the Host ascended into the heavens.

Such a tiny thing, this orb of light, it fell from the sky and landed on a small island somewhere in the middle of the world. It lay like the lost treasury it was expected to be. Except it was not really lost, only waiting. A small glowing marble of importance.

She skipped through the grasses and explored every pretty flower she saw. At eight years of age, every clump of weeds, every tall tree, and every small mound of earth or hidden burrow was something to be investigated. Something to be studied, not for its intent or purpose, but for its sheer wonder.

She sat to rest from her play in the shadow of the rumbling mountain that was the backdrop of her home, and watched a tiny dragonfly dance among the garden foliage.

Her mother looked out the window from the back of their house to check on her and smiled seeing her daughter rolling, singing and playing on the lawn. Like her child, she was raised on this idyllic isle with the majestic waves to the south and the equally impressive peak to the north.

Her people had a story about the mountain. It was said to be the home of the old gods, and that you could always tell when they were in residence by the way it trembled and shook the earth. It was a story as old as all memories and gave reassurance to the islanders, not the fear one might expect from living so near to a slumbering giant. Although it must have formed this very chain of islands with its once molten breath, that was long ago, and had not in living memory done more than shake a picture or two from a wall.

The small child got on her knees to look at the tiny little insect, a beautiful dragonfly that fluttered in front of her. "Hello," she said.

And the buzzing of the delicate wings replied, "Hello little one. Who are you?"

Delighted the little girl said, "Elena. I am a princess."

"Do tell?"

"My mother said that her grandmother's grandmother, a long time ago, was a princess too, so that makes me a princess. Right?"

"Indeed it does little one, I knew your grandfather from long ago when he meet her. She loved the sea and he was the sea," the petite Dragon buzzed.

"What's your name?" Elena asked.

"I be stAkArAl. Seventeenth of the Fallen from the Seventh Rise. And I give what is mine to give. I have a secret to show you. Do you want to see it?"

"Oh yes, I can keep a secret."

"This is not a secret for you to keep, but something for you to give back to the world," the dragonfly said as it took flight and led her to a nearby bounty of flowers that had sprung up and gave great beauty to the field.

The little girl looked at the very center of the impromptu bed of bright blue Daisies, yellow Surprise Lilies and tiny bouquets of Baby's Breath and saw a small glowing orb that twinkled and glistened in the light. She reached in and picked up the treasure. "It's the most pretty thing I have ever seen," she said. "What's it for?"

"To heal the world's pain," the dragonfly said.

"What do I do with it?" Elena asked.

"Cast it into the water's edge where the mountain smokes and the waters dance."

Elena stood up and began walking, then running towards the beach. She laughed as the sand squeezed between her toes as she ran along the shore towards the mountain.

"Here?" she asked stopping at the point where she was told never to go beyond for the danger was just over there where the mountain gave itself to the sea in a long slow march of blackened earth with veins of deep red.

"Here is fine little one," buzzed the answer.

She looked at the glowing orb and then raising her arm as high into the air as her little arm could reach, she flung it into the water that steamed up from the unseen, but ever present flow of molten earth that constantly extended the edge of the land. The surface of the water erupted into flame as the orb touched it. The land trembled and the sky darkened. Lava thrashed and tossed ash into the air. Lightning flashed through the immediate dark clouds that had appeared. A strong wind filled the space as water, earth, fire and air all merged to become one.

"Elena!" the sound of her mother's frantic voice caused the little girl to turn. She pointed to where she had tossed the orb and told her mother, "I did it mother, I ended the world's pain."

Sweeping her up in her arms, Elena's mother hugged her tightly and then looked out at where the child was pointing. She saw nothing save for the eternal sea as it pressed up alongside the silent mountain against the clear blue sky. She sat the girl down upon the sand and taking her hand, led her back towards the house. "You know you are not supposed to leave the yard," she scolded the girl.

" stAkArAl, my friend told me it was ok. He is a Dragonfly."

Her mother struggled to keep a stern face as she chuckled. "If we all had a Dragon as a friend, and your Innocence, we might just end the world's pain my love. It's time to eat, let's go home."

Rebirth
Nova Creatio
Children of Tiamate
Epilogue

The hardened lava, earthen rock and metal melted by fire, cooled by air and polished by water, became, once again, that black obsidian mirror that reflected a singular will forced on the world, shown upon its smooth surface. The shards of the self-created once again made whole, un-shattered by hilt. The many reflections of the speck now bound together as one insignificant instance without a means to escape. Rage contained. Lust, greed, fear, anger and betrayal removed from the world, contained in the blackness of an image that reflected nothing of substance back.

The earth trembled and the heavens flashed as the wound was healed. Rock and sand, mud and sea flowed up as starry skies and misty clouds rained down. Fire met each as all were caught in the wind and merged. With this reversal, the sky and earth, water and fire became one. And that which created by violent force was given peace and completeness. The oneness returned as the forced creation was un-created. The Void was whole and Tiamate was reborn taking back each of its children.

And the universe was once again without form, and Void; and darkness was upon the face of the deep. And a Spirit moved upon the face of the waters that was the deep void. A wind, a breath from something beyond the Void blew.

The breath carried forth a meaning, "Let there be light." And behold there was light.

There was no anger, fear, pain or violence, only peace and a new creation did the Void become.

And it was good.

The End and Beginning

Storm Front
by Randy A. Cook

The wind chimes on the front porch of the turn of the century farmhouse gently whispered out their soft notes for the home's occupants to hear. Nothing complex, just random notes, singing a random song, on this random day. The sound would have been considered calming, even relaxing, if the family living here had the time to sit on that old wooden porch and enjoy them. But not today, no sitting, no time for the simpler things. The wheat in the fields had turned the expected golden yellow hue and needed to be harvested. No harvest, no land payment, no money for the rest of the year, no food, no heat, no shelter and of course no cash for the next planting. The endless cycle of life, that needs to be repeated year after year. A fragile rhythm that has been playing out for generations and is expected to continue for many more. Maybe it is not so fragile after all, having survived for so many years and it just seems delicate in the course of each day. Maybe it is all a matter of perspective.

Walter was out in the implement yard working on the combine, again. Ruth, his wife, was by his side handing him a wrench, or a screwdriver, and sometimes a crowbar. Their youngest son, Larry, was scrambling all over the massive machine. He was not really accomplishing much, except in his own mind. He would jump down from the cab and ask what he could do next to help, and his parents would patiently assign him yet another humdrum task that he would immediately attend to. "Clean out the headers," his dad would say, and the boy bolted to the front of the harvester and started pulling out the dried and hollow stems of the plants that had been feed into the machine when it broke and failed to be augured into the bowel of the device for winnowing. All the while, he would carefully watch his father repair the broken machine knowing that someday he would be the one under that piece of equipment trying his best to get it back up and out in the field.

The crackling and hissing of the radio that was setting on a nearby pile of tractor tires caused his mother to turn and slowly rotate the knob back and forth trying to tune the local station in. "The storm front continues to move in from the south. Heavy rains are expected with a chance of pea size hail. The National Weather Bureau has issued a Thunder Storm warning for the entire tri-county area until 1:00am. Stay tuned for additional information as it develops."

Walter was doing his best to beat the storm, or to at least out run it long enough to get the crops in. Harvest time was always a race. Racing against the weather, racing against exhaustion, racing against the bank and its unrelenting loan payment. Always that same rhythm. The not so steady beat that those who have never had to live within its deafening sound mistakenly call the simple life.

Crawling out from under the ageing combine, Walter calls to Larry, "Son, go pull the grain truck out of the pole barn." Wiping some of the grease from his hands on to a torn up rag, the tired farmer looked up at the southern sky and the darkening clouds gathering in the distance.

"You get it fixed dear?" Ruth asked already knowing that her husband of thirty years would not have come out from under that piece of equipment without success.

"Yeah, I got it patched back up. But it's only a patch, with any luck it will hold until we can get that field finished up. After that, this winter, I will either see if I can overhaul it or talk to the bank about getting something newer."

"I knew you could fix it," Ruth said, always confident in her man's ability to overcome such things. No doubts at all, sometimes that faith was the only thing that kept Walter going. He loved his wife.

Larry dashed excitedly for the pole barn to do as instructed. Now, even Larry knew that at his age, you were supposed to have a license to drive a vehicle, even a beat up old grain truck like this. But things were different on the farm. Everybody pitched in at harvest time, regardless of what the law said. It would be Larry's responsibility to move the truck to the end of the wheat field and have it setting in the right spot, so that when his dad would circle the field gathering up the wheat until the combine's bin was full, he could dump that load into the waiting truck. Walter would have no loss of time having to move the truck himself each time. It was a simple but important job. When he was younger, it was his mother who would drive the truck. Larry could still remember the first time his dad assigned him this task. He was no longer just a child, but a real contributing farm hand. Larry could move the truck every 100 yards or so and have it in position for his dad. Never once would he be allowed to put that old truck in anything other than "granny" gear. In granny gear, the truck would at first lurch forward as Larry eased his foot off of the clutch, and then the old truck would slowly inch forward in a more or less straight line along the edge of the field until it was in just the right spot to take on the next load the combine would dump into its bed. Clutch, lurch, inch, repeat. That was Larry's job.

If anyone had the time to listen, they would have heard the notes of the wind chime on the front porch ring out just a bit louder and it's song just a touch faster.

The powerful machine roared to life as Walter turned over the diesel engine. He let it idle for a bit, listening to the sound of the firing pistons. Now the true test, he pulled back on a large lever and slowly released the hand-grip that engaged the header; the front of the implement sprang to life. Its massive revolving reel began to spin and the knife cutter bar chopped back and forth... just as they were supposed to. He held his breath for just a bit as everything held together. Putting the combine in gear, he headed to the nearby field to finish his work before the coming storm finished it for him. He glanced over his shoulder out the backside window to see Ruth waving "bye" to him. Turning his attention to the task and path ahead, he moved into the field.

Larry was driving the grain truck along the edge of the field heading to the appropriate spot when the combine caught up and then passed him. It was a race from Larry's perception; a race he would not win while in granny gear, but he was determined to give it his best shot. Win or lose, he would be right where he was supposed to be when the time came. So intent was he on the imagined high-speed race that he did not notice how dark and close the clouds were to them. It was not until a distant flash of lightning caught his attention that he even noticed the coming storm.

Ruth was back at the farmhouse brewing some tea. She knew that the summer heat combined with the cloud of dust, pollen and wheat chaff that always accompanied the harvest would make her boys thirsty. The answer, iced tea. It was still hot and the approaching storm, with its humidity, made the air sticky and muggy. Same answer as before, iced tea. To be honest, brewing tea, was not exactly what she was doing. Even on a rural farm, the lure of instant tea to make such a necessity was a quick and easy solution. Getting the exact ratio of tea, sugar and ice was the hard part.

As she perfected her magical tonic the radio crackled and hissed, but the announcer was still easily heard, "This is an update from the National Weather Bureau. The storm front moving into the area has been upgraded to a Severe Thunder Storm. Golf ball size hail has been reported in the town of Coffeyville. The storm continues to advance in a north eastern direction with multiple storm lines moving up from Oklahoma."

Coffeyville was about an hour and half to the southwest. Ruth stirred her pitcher of tea a bit faster as the wind chimes outside matched her pace.

Larry watched the combine circle the field. Each time it passed, he could taste the thick haze of discarded husk and heavy dust spewed out from the back of the combine. He wore a handkerchief over his mouth as his mother had suggested, but it did little to stop the choking cloud that filled his nose and stung his eyes. He had always found the best solution was to dart down the drainage ditch that bound the field and sit at the tree line on the other side until his dad had passed, and then to make a mad dash back up the incline to the truck before he was needed.

The taste of the dirt in the air was not exactly a bad taste as it filled each breath; it was a sort of plain taste, not sweet, or salty or even sour or bitter, just plain. If musky was a flavor, that would be the closest thing to describe it. It was more the texture as it landed on your lips and coated your tongue that caught your attention, and that you could not avoid. A gritty feeling that no matter how hard you tried to wet your lips or wipe from the front of your teeth, it always remained. An irritant that you just could not spit out of your mouth. Now the dust, that was a different matter, it weighed on your lungs with each breath and stung your eyes. The watering eyes you could get used to, but the heaviness inside you, in your lungs, no amount of coughing could get rid of that. It was with you until the harvest was done for the day and you could sleep it off.

Only once did he see the combine stop at the far end of the field. The trail of stubble spewed onto the ground paused and the thick veil of dust stopped and was carried off by an ever-increasing wind. His dad jumped from the cab of the implement to make some adjustment to the belts on the side of it. "Dang belts always coming off," he parroted the words he could only imagine his father saying as he pried, pushed, pulled and cursed the belt back into place.

"This should be the round he will need to unload," Larry said to himself as he got behind the wheel of the old grain truck and eased it out of neutral and into low. Clutch, lurch, inch, and in no time at all he was in the right place.

A clap of thunder surprised him and he looked up into the dark sky that had closed in on the wheat field. He glanced across the field to once again see the stubble flying and the dust plume rising into the air. Belt in place, father in cab, and combine once again chewing its way through the wheat on its journey to the dumping point where the old grain truck was parked.

Pulling the combine up beside the truck, Walter stepped out onto a narrow ledge that ran the length of the machine and swung a broad pipe out from the combine's holding bin and over the back of the truck bed. The wind was starting to blow so hard that he had trouble latching it into place. After a brief struggle with a lynch pin, the pipe was positioned and the auger was turned on. Larry climbed into the back of the truck with a wide shovel and as the grain was emptied from the combine and rushed out of the pipe, he would push it towards the corners and sides of the space. If he thought the dust was bad just standing on the side of the field when the combine passed, it was nothing compared to the blinding swirl that washed around him now. But what had to be done, had to be done. He was glad that his mom had insisted that he wear the bandana around his mouth.

With the bin emptied and the truck now almost full, he looked over to see his mother walking over to his father and handing him a tall glass of iced tea. She turned towards him, smiled and waved him down. He knew that she had a glass for him as well.

A quick jump and feet on the ground, he ran over to his parents. His dad was covered in dust, sweat, grease and just a touch of dried blood on his knuckles. No air conditioner in this old combine, just a fan that clogged up more than it blew any air. But at the moment, air conditioning was a low priority, for the wind had picked up with a vengeance and the heat of the day was giving way to the chill of an arriving storm.

Standing at the field's edge, Walter sipped his iced tea as he watched the darkening sky. The clouds hung heavy above him, some dipping dangerously low to the earth. Storms are certainly no strangers to these horizons, every season they would come and go. But like all strangers, they each carry their own secrets, their own unexpected twists and turns. Walter was concerned about what secrets this storm carried and would soon reveal. He swished a gulp of his tea around in his mouth in an attempt to wash the grit from his teeth and spit the now polluted drink onto the ground.

"Larry, get the truck up to the house," Walter said to his son, "...and make it fast."

Lightening was flashing across the sky, not against the horizon, but in the very air above their heads. The wind was blowing hard, churning the clouds in ways that made both Walter and Ruth very nervous.

"What about the rest of the wheat still standing out there?" Larry gestured towards the remaining uncut field. "Larry... the truck... now!"

The tone in his father's voice struck Larry as strange. He heard something not so much in his words, but between his words, his gestures, that he was... unaccustomed to hearing, fear. Larry knew that today was the day he got to get out of granny gear.

The combine with its header elevated high enough to avoid any low growing shrubs, rumbled along the half gravel, half dirt, half road, half path, towards the house at a pace it was rarely allowed. The trees lining the way were leaning and swaying in a wild fashion. Many of the trees were decades old with thick and heavy trunks; branches stretched high over the top of the combine as it made haste to the supposed safety of the implement yard. Those long old wooden arms that had sheltered the road for many years whipped back and forth. The fact that the tops of these massive trees could be so easily moved by the invisible hand of the wind disturbed Walter. "I should have trimmed those things last fall," he worried, knowing that one quick snap could do massive damage requiring expensive repairs to a combine that was already on its last leg. His wife always said that he beat himself up over things that were really out of his control and in the hands of God. She was not wrong.

Ruth climbed into the cab of the old grain truck, on the passenger side. This simple act was not lost on Larry who was behind the wheel. He lifted one foot from the clutch while keeping even pressure on the brake, then moving it to the accelerator. Clutch, lurch, inch, now back to the clutch as he fumbled with the gearshift. The grinding of gears was all he heard or more accurately felt as he fought the lever moving it into second gear. Clutch and lurch, but this time a bit faster than before. Granny gear was a thing of the past. Larry looked nervously out the windshield as he watched his father in the combine pulling away from him.

"You can do this," his mother offered gently by his side.

Clutch, and with a bit less fumbling, third gear was found along with the speed that was needed. It was darker than he had ever seen it before at this time of day. Larry reached for and pulled on the switch to turn on the headlights. Already juggling the clutch, brake and accelerator with his feet, he stretched one of his legs and tried blindly to find the high beam toggle switch on the floor, not daring to look down for fear of losing his thin grasp on the path ahead.

His mother was more concerned with the heavy branches hanging overhead than Larry was. He was more focused on keeping the truck on the path to the house. He was responsible for the load of grain and was determined to get it into the barn safe and sound. The wheel, which lacked power steering, was hard enough to turn and the force of the wind just made it more difficult as he climbed the steep incline on the way home, and fought to make the turn, which was of course, halfway up the hill. Ordinarily, the turn while in the slow motion of granny gear and in the full light of day was not a concern, right now, however, it was terrifying with the wind, the shadows and a speed just beyond what he was accustom to.

There was a loud thundering crack just overhead that made both Larry and his mother jump. It was not clear if the deafening sound was the clap of nearby lightning or the breaking of the tree limb that collapsed onto the hood of the truck. In reflex, Larry slammed on the brake, but without stepping on the clutch, the vehicle continued to lumber forward in an awkward sputtering fashion. The limb slammed against the windshield causing spider like cracks across the entire window until the broken branch fell to the way side and the truck continued on.

"Keep going son, the windshield is nothing. Getting the truck up to the barn is the only thing that matters."

Larry had walked, run, skipped, and rode his bike up this same hill hundreds of times in the past, but now, driving this truck, with this grain, in the dwindling day light made it seem like a strange and threatening terrain that he had never encountered before. He leaned forward, white knuckles on the wheel, squinting his eyes, looking through the shattered glass to find his way home. The rain that had just started did not make the task any easier. The windshield wipers, had they worked, would have been useless on the distorted and broken surface A waste of time even if he had been brave enough to search for the on/off switch.

Walter could see the headlights of the grain truck in his rear view mirror as he worked to get this piece of machinery back up to the yard. The wind pressed against the large awkwardly shaped implement in an unrelenting effort to push it off the road and into the gully at the wayside. The rain had started; this was a good thing for the most part. As long as it was just a touch of rain, it meant that nothing else more troubling was nearby. It was then that he heard the tiny dings on the cab of the combine that he recognized as the falling of hail; he pressed the old combine for just a bit more speed. He once again looked back and was relieved see the grain truck and his family following behind him. "We are almost to the house," he thought to himself.

Ruth heard the ice hitting the truck and saw it falling in the road reflecting small pea sized glints of brightness in the headlights. "Hail," she thought to herself, "not a good sign." She watched the lights on the combine turn into the implement yard up ahead of them. "Almost there."

"Stop in the yard and find out what your father wants us to do," she told her son. Larry nodded in response, relieved that somebody else would be telling him what to do next.

By the time that Larry pulled the old "51" into the implement yard, his dad was out of the combine and running over to the truck. The rain had almost stopped or more accurately was replaced by hailstones that were growing in size with each passing moment.

Opening the driver's side door of the truck cab, Walter reached in and helped or maybe pulled would be a better description, Larry from the seat. Ruth already had her door open and was getting down from the cab. Larry stood for a moment, and watched in fascination, the low hanging clouds as they nearly touched the earth just beyond the barn. Walter pushed Larry towards his mother. "Get to the house while I put this away," he instructed his son as he climbed up into the cab and put the truck effortlessly into gear. He sped towards the barn while Ruth and Larry headed for the farmhouse. On the rushing of the wind, you could hear the wind chimes on the porch greeting the family with an erratic clinking of metal hitting metal and the dinging out of half notes in a wild and frantic fashion.

By the time Walter made it back to the house, drenched in rain water, and slightly bruised by the hail, Ruth was listening intently to the announcer on the Radio, "A tornado watch has been issued for the Labette and Neosho counties effective immediately. All residence should seek immediate shelter."

Ruth, who was sitting at the table, looked up at Walter, back towards the radio, then back up at her husband. Larry was standing by the window looking out at the lightning as it raced across the sky. Walter nodded his head, touched her hand and said, "Get to

Cellar!" Without hesitation, she got up, took Larry by the hand and headed towards the back door.

The cellar wasn't big, only about twelve feet in length and maybe six feet wide. It was mostly buried in the yard behind the house. It was old, very old. It was on the farm when they had bought the place. Larry often thought that it looked like something abandoned, an ancient Aztec tomb from a long lost city. He was a kid, so he was allowed such fanciful ideas. It was made of old course concrete, only a couple of feet of its rounded cement top protruded from the mound of earth that surrounded it. Larry would often play on the top of what he thought of as a smooth mountain. It made an excellent launching pad for his bike. He and his friends would push their bikes to the top and then race down the mound of earth gathering more speed than they ever could muster by peddling. In the winter, when it was covered in ice and snow, it was even better. The inside of the cellar was dark, dank and smelled of old onions and dirt. The door into the underground cell was heavy and always took great effort to open. Larry had no idea how hard that door would be to close or open from within, because every time he would go down the steps to this murky place, they always left the door open. On one side of the narrow bunker were shelves packed with jars that contained the fruits and vegetables that his mother had canned. He never understood why she took so much time every year to can and pickle these things since you can get any and all of the same things from the local grocery store. When he would ask both his mother and father, they would always say that it tasted better than the store bought stuff. Larry could never tell the difference. On the other side hung onions and lots of different herbs bound in upside down clumps. Potatoes filled the bins below. Larry liked the herbs; they tasted and smelled nice, but the onions were another story. He did not like, nor would he eat, an onion store bought or otherwise.

On the ceiling, at the very center of this half-buried room, was a round hole about one foot in diameter. His father had built a sort of iron cap that fit down into the hole to cover it. It had a rounded lid that would prevent any rain from getting in, but had openings on its side that let in light. With the storm outside, there really was not much light to let in.

Once inside, his mother took out a battery-powered lantern that they kept down there and turned it on. They were lucky that it worked! Larry had on more than one occasion, left it on while messing around down here. Exploring, was the way he had explained it to his parents when confronted about it. Luck was with them tonight. So he and his mother sat down on some crates stored at the far end of the cellar away from the door, light in hand, and waited for his father to join them. Larry was hungery and started to wonder about opening one of those jars of peaches.

It did not take long for Walter to join them in the dimly lit underground. He tossed Ruth a blanket that he had picked up from the house on his way out. He stood on the top stair and watched the storm outside. Just beyond the barn, not far at all, he watched as the clouds dragged the earth that was the pasture or maybe even as close as the implement yard. The dark clouds began to swirl and lightning flashed high and low in the sky. The cellar was not too far from the house and Walter could still see the lights shining from the kitchen windows. He had worked hard to make that house livable. When they first moved out here, that old farmhouse was not suitable for any respectable man, let alone his family. It took several months, bordering on a year, of hard labor to get that old building into a suitable condition for his family. He looked at the upstairs windows that he had just replaced and remembered that long weekend of tearing out the old and installing the new. Just windows, he thought to himself. The house lights began to flicker and then went dark. There was no doubt in his mind; it was here.

Larry could hear the sound from the outside as his mother put the blanket over his shoulders. It was a long low roar, almost a growl. To him it sounded like some distant creature on the hunt. Hunting for the weak, the wounded or the young. He thought that he could hear the wind chimes on the front porch ringing out in an erratic and frightened pattern. A warning perhaps to anyone that might hear it. A call to run and hide for something was coming and it was hungry. Some great beast with fierce beating wings that battered those not yet hidden. Larry was hidden, at the bottom of a buried cellar and under the cover of his blanket. No Dragon would find him here.

In the flashing of the lightning, Walter saw a heavy darkness rising up from implement yard as the clouds no longer acted like clouds. Instead of floating in the air or even passing close to the ground, they stabbed with violence hard at the soil and tore at the earth and all that sat upon it. Walter saw the sharp winds spinning in that ominous pattern that he had always feared and could see the debris flying through the air.

Walter pulled the heavy cellar door closed and slid the sturdy deadbolt into place securing the door; locking them inside and the storm outside. He stepped back to the center of the room and looked up at the capped hole in the ceiling. The thin slits on the sides of the lid flashed as the lightning from the storm outside raged and threatened to enter in.

The door of the cellar started to shake, but the deadbolt and hinges held... for the moment. The iron cap that covered the hole in the ceiling started to whistle as the air rushed through it. Even though the iron cap was wedged tightly into the hole, Larry remembered his father pounding it into place with a sledgehammer, it started to slowly twist and shudder as if whatever was outside wanted inside. And it thought it had found an entrance.

The sound was no longer a low growl, but rather like that of a massive train railing above and below; it was all around. It screamed and demanded attention. Demanded entrance. Demanded a sacrifice. But the walls of the old cellar and the blanket over Larry's shoulders remained strong and resisted the assault of the hungry beast outside despite its best efforts to devour them. Larry's mother sat in silence that contradicted the storm as she pulled him just a bit closer to her side. Larry's father stood at the center of the cellar, ready to stop whatever came through that door or the hole in the ceiling no matter what the cost or in vain the effort.

Suddenly, there was the sound of things, many things, hitting the cellar door. A pounding that echoed through the room. This was immediately followed by the heavy slamming of bits and pieces against the cellar cap that rang out with a dull metal against metal sound. It resonated in the room until the shelves of jars and pounds of potatoes dulled the hard sharp sound.

All at once, just when Larry was sure that it would burst through their cellar walls, it stopped... nothing... no sound, no pounding, no screaming wind. Was it gone, or was it waiting?

After several minutes of complete silence from the outside, Walter looked to his wife and then tried to open the cellar door. Sliding the deadbolt back and with the normal push that Walter had expected to finish the job, the door did not move. He had to put his shoulder into it and apply some real force in the effort. The sound of boards, glass and tin could be heard falling away as it finally swung open to the outside. After a brief survey of the landscape beyond the confines of the cellar, Walter helped Ruth, and then Larry, step clear of the darkness.

Much to his relief, Larry saw his home still standing before him. He was worried that it had all been taken. In fact, Walter and Ruth were relieved as well, although they would have never let Larry know of their fear. He could once again hear the soft gentle sounds of the wind chimes from the front porch as they called out to him that all was safe.

It wasn't until Larry turned around and saw his father staring at what was left of the barn that his heart missed a beat. Larry followed his father as they walked out back, towards the implement yard.

His dad did not say a word as he saw the twisted shape of the combine wrapped around the trees at the far side of the yard, or the sheets of tin that lay spewed across the nearby field from where they had been ripped from the barn. Even the pile of tires had been tossed from here to the pond.

Walter walked to the side of the barn where he had parked the old grain truck with its load of wheat. The truck lay on its side and the grain, what was left of it, was littered across the ground. He looked over, saw that the silo had basically been ripped from the ground, and tossed aside, spilling the contents over what must have been a quarter of a mile.

They both turned and walked slowly back to the house where they found Ruth picking up trash and debris from the yard. Ruth looked up from her work as they approached and Walter shook his head. She straightened herself up and went into the house to see about starting dinner.

The next few days were pretty much a blur. The sheriff and emergency vehicles showed up at some point, followed by some insurance adjusters and lots of well meaning neighbors. Larry watched them come and go and helped where he could, picking up tin, barb wire and pieces of the combine.

They had a tuna noodle casserole that night brought over by Mrs. Smith who lived in the house about a quarter of a mile to the south. Her husband helped Larry's dad pull the tractor out of the hedgerow. The night after that it was a beef casserole from the Carsons and after that, it was turkey sandwiches from the Wilsons. All good neighbors, all really good food. Not as good as his mother's home cooking Larry thought, but she was pretty busy trying to put things back together after the storm.

Even with friends and neighbors' helping, clean up was slow and could only go so far without that all-important thing called money. The combine needed replacing, lumber is required to repair the barn, the fences, the sheds, and the old grain truck was going to need a lot to get it back up and running. But fixing it would be cheaper than replacing it.

It was about a week later that the family all put on their Sunday best and rode into town. Larry's father, never liked going into town much, he always said he would never live there and that it would eat you alive if you let it. Amazingly enough, the pickup truck had escaped much of the damage to their homestead with little more than a few dents and dings from hail damage. After the hour-long drive, they pulled up in front of the grey-bricked building of the bank and parked. The bricks reminded Larry of the scales of some long dead lizard and he thought it overly tall and stood like a menacing structure. Maybe that was the intent, to intimidate those who approached it. Larry thought the wide front doors with its great white marble pillars looked like teeth with a gaping throat behind them. The second story windows looked like eyes staring down upon the street below, as if the monster building was selecting its next meal.

Larry sat in the waiting room and watched his parents through the glass walls of the office that bore the name "Loan Department" on the door. The chairs were plush enough, but he was still uncomfortable sitting in them and waiting. He would switch from chair to chair, but they were all the same, comfortable but uncomfortable.

He watched his parents through the glass walls of the office, unable to hear a single word being said. And that, just made him ever more fidgety, and he would switch to a different seat. After what seemed like hours in silence, he saw his father getting visibly agitated as the man in the suit on the other side of the big black desk just continued to shake his head side to side. He watched as his mother touched his father's arm and calm was returned. After a bit more talking and a bit more head shaking, he saw his parents stand and head back his way. "Finally," he thought. "We can go home."

Larry stood and looked into his parents' faces trying to figure out what was said behind those glass walls just beyond his ear shot. He wanted his parents to take him from this monster of a building.

His mother took him by his hand and said, "We need to get home so we can pack son, we have a new adventure ahead of us."

His Father led them from the building to start something new. The meaning of his mother's words were clear and Larry now understood that the storm was not the only Dragon that they had faced. Surviving one only to be eaten by another. Beasts often hunt in packs. One to frighten, distract and wound you, while the other waits, stalks and tries to takes you down, an ambush of a scavenger. This was something he would never forget, regardless of what came next. It would take more than a pair of monsters to stop the not so fragile rhythm of life. He would have to remember to pack the wind chimes from the porch and to listen to them more carefully the next time something came a hunting.

The End

The Sinking of the Titanic
(A story from New Genesis)

By Randy A. Cook

"From my memories and adventures of the time I spent on the wayward world of New Genesis while living among its strange inhabitants. This recollection occurred shortly after my initial abduction and imprisonment on this world of hidden technological miracles that allowed its people's lives and dreams to be one and the same without consequences or accountability." - Christopher Havok

The ship was long and sleek, black in color, edged in gold and silver with two tall masts trimmed to catch the wind as the battle raged. The icy waters hit high against the sides of the galley as it cut through the waves attempting to out maneuver the beast that slashed through the northern seas with its floating islands of ice and snow.

A strong gale blew the icy mist of the sea and a falling torrent of sleet and rain over the entire horrific scene. Only Sword Cross Chance, the Captain of this vessel, knew for sure, if the storm was the result of the mighty beating of the wings of the Ice Dragon as it savagely attached the boat, or if it was the result of Sword's attempt to create a proper backdrop for the entire event.

To all who called New Genesis home, the massive and mysterious machinery and mechanics buried deep beneath the surface of this little moon, responded to the inhabitants' every wish and desire by making the impossible possible and the possible, as a general rule, absurd.

"To the death," shouted Sword Cross Chance at the Ice Dragon from his perch on one of the sailing mast. He was about to make additional calls for the creature's demise but was distracted by the approach of a flying craft.

From some hidden pocket in his long coat with tails, Sword produced and stretched out a beautiful brass looking glass, and directed it towards the craft as it grew near. He saw a large aircraft fashioned after a bleached beached behemoth of a whale gently pull up alongside of the magnificent sailing vessel, which continued to be locked in the heated battle with the great frozen sea monster.

Collapsing and returning the looking glass to his pocket, Sword Cross Chance ordered that the gangplank be extended. Taking hold of a guide rope hanging from the top of one of the sails. he quickly and quite elegantly swung down to the deck below a few feet from the plank to greet his new guests.

"Romeo Red, my dear fellow. I thought that was you. Welcome to my humble endeavor," Sword said as he watched two figures disembark from the albino aircraft and walk the plank onto the ship.

"I saw the commotion as I was flying by and just had to stop in and see what you were about," replied Romeo Red with a deep low bow accompanied by a grand flourish of the arm and a flare of the hand. "You remember my protégé, Christopher... something."

"Havok, Christopher Havok," the boy beside him said in a flat tone. "And a hostage, since a kidnapping would be a better description of what's going on here." Then looking to the right and then to his left at the chaos occurring all around as pirates were being thrown this way and that by a Dragon, he asked, "What IS going on here?"

"The boy has a point," Romeo echoed. "What is going on here?"

"So glad you asked my friend, after all, you are in no small way responsible for this endeavor."

Romeo Red ever so slightly bowed his head in humble acknowledgement of his obvious achievement. "Do tell."

"You, my dear Red, are a great source of inspiration to us all around here with your scholarly study of the Earth and its inhabitants," Sword Cross Chance cast a glance at Christopher. "With you as my example, I have meticulously studied this event in Earth's history, and have created this exact reproduction of one of its greatest battles... The sinking of the Titanic." Sword spoke with a great sense of accomplishment as he now looked around at the poor pirates being ripped apart by the ice sickle fangs of the Dragon that was terrorizing the sailors.

"Imagine if you will, or simply look around at my creation, the steely eyed and handsome Captain of the greatest pirate ship ever to sail the 8 and 1/2 half seas. That part is obviously played by me. As he valiantly leads his daring crew," Sword paused briefly to step out of the way as the severed bloodied head of one of the crew was flung at him by the Ice Dragon, before he continues," on the good ship, *The Unsinkable Molly Brown*, as it hunted down to do battle with the Great Dragon Titanic." It was the Dragon's turn to pause from the carnage it was inflicting to wave politely to Romeo Red and Christopher Havok."

"Molly Brown was a survivor of the Titanic and...," Christopher tried to explain.

"Of course she was a survivor. She had to survive. For this was a monumental death match with the Greatest Dragon of your time. The very survival of the human race, as you know it, depended on her surviving," Sword Cross Chance interrupted as he raised his gloved fist and shook it defiantly at the Dragon who had returned to dismembering and devouring the crew. "It is so very gratifying to hear confirmation of my re-creation's authenticity from someone who was an actual witness to this great Earth battle." Sword wiped a tear from his eye.

"I wasn't there," Christopher attempted to explain. "And the Titanic was actually..."

"Enough about you," Sword Cross Chance cut Christopher off. "Now back to my historical account."

Nearby, a pirate sets fire to his own hair and runs screaming towards the great Ice Dragon.

"What an interesting thing to do," Romeo Red said to Sword Cross Chance as he watched the spectacle of the man with melting hair dash to and fro in a zigzag pattern towards the Beast. "What's the point?"

Sword Cross Chance lifted his head ever so slightly and with a finger of authority waved his hand at the sailor. "To frighten the Dragon of course," Sword replied. "It is well documented that an Ice Dragon's fear of fire would render him paralyzed in the face of such heroic courage."

"Ahhh," said Romeo Red. "That makes sense... but how do you explain that?" he said pointing to the events unfolding immediately before them.

The Pirate, screaming in pain at the top of his lungs, with hair a blazing, and fear glazed eyes, was stopped dead in his tracks as the Ice Dragon turned its massive head and blasted him with its blizzard breath. The Beast exhaled a mighty pant of frigid blowing snow that turned the Pirate, blazing hair and all, into a solid statue of ice. Then with a flick of its massive tail, the Dragon smashed the frozen pirate into a thousand shard of ice that scattered across the deck of *The Unsinkable Molly Brown*.

Cup in hand, Sword Cross Chance, studied the many broken pieces of the pirate and selected several choice chunks of ice. He promptly dropped the cubes into his glass of what was now a properly prepared Pirate's Cove Iced Rum cocktail. "Obviously this particular Ice Dragon has absolutely no respect for history."

Christopher Havok simply shakes his head as he turns and steps over the ice of what used to a flaming haired pirate. He was returning to Romeo's ship.

A sand barge appeared behind the ship with a solitary figure sitting in a lawn chair upon it. She reached up and adjusted the overly large beach umbrella that sheltered her from the bright sun, the torrent of the ice storm, and the blood and guts of the slaughtered sailors that rained down all around her.

"Magnificent," she proclaimed as she watched the battle. "So real, so natural, so... so... dramatic! Did I say Magnificent?"

"Mace Righteous!" Sword Cross Chance exclaimed. "That is still what you are calling yourself isn't it?"

"Of course it is my dashing Sword. It suits me I think. Don't you?" She rose from her lawn chair and levitated to the deck to be nearer to her fellows.

"A beautiful weapon by any other name... or something like that. But as long as the word 'Beautiful' is used, it certainly fits you my love." Sword Cross Chance replied.

"Romeo, Romeo, my oh so Red Romeo," Mace Righteous said as she saw Romeo Red standing on the deck. "This must be an extraordinary event to pull even you from your dusty libraries. And how do your studies go? Still toiling away in your quest for our dearly depart home world, Ert?"

"Earth," he corrected her. "And yes, my work to uncover the mysteries of that far away place continues. To be honest though, it is not yet so dear or departed. "

"Oh? when last we talked I thought you said that the star it circled was about to go boom."

"It is indeed nearing that point, but not yet. Which is why my research is so very important, for soon, there won't be anything left to research. I believe that I have timed our arrival just before the nova, so maybe 'far away' is even a stretch."

"Well that is so very interesting Romeo," Mace said tilting her head towards Sword Cross Chance as he knelt over a selection of long pointed lances.

"What do you think of this one?" Sword Cross Chance asked as he selected and lifted for their approval a long deadly harpoon with a curved barb on the end with its razor sharp point. Embedded in the head of the lance was a large Ruby Red Stone that glowed in the reflected light of the ice storm. The harpoon was weighted down at the back end far below the handgrips to give it a lethal balance when thrust.

"A fine selection. But is it authentic?" asked Romeo Red.

"From my extensive observations and detailed examination of the historical facts," Sword replied. "Each of these weapons would fit the description of the item used to deliver the coup-de-grace. Notice the fine detail of the device, a somewhat delicate tip at the top, but given deadly intent with its girth hidden below the surface, if you will, of the Champion that will drive it home splitting the creature in half.

"Well done!" Mace Righteous exclaimed clapping her hands together in delight.

As they continued to debate the weapon of choice that Sword would use, a quartet of Pirates advanced on the Ice Dragon from the upper deck of the ship in yet another attempt to slay it. Each of the Pirates carried with him a weapon selected to do the most harm thought possible to the creature. Sword Cross Chance had armed these men based on his early research. The first carried what Sword called a Violin. This was a menacing construct that could be used as both a stabbing instrument or if the need arose, as short-ranged bow launching a narrow arrow that always accompanied the device. The second pirate brought to the squeamish something similarly dangerous called a Cello. Its large size made it perfect as a battering ram with a devilishly clever steel point at the bottom. The third weapon was a Viola. This may be the most difficult of the weapons to utilize since it required the user to get close enough to garrote the victim with one of the four strings it held. The fourth weapon, which Sword Cross Chance admitted he had no understanding as to how it was to be used, was something called a harmonica.

In unison, they assaulted the Dragon. The strike carried with it a marching music that dramatically increased the suspense of the attack. Admittedly, the strange sounds given off by the pirates and their collection of antique weapons did indeed give the Ice Dragon pause, but only for a moment, and then he swallowed them whole. The harmonica apparently got caught in its teeth and gave off the oddest sounds each time the Dragon either inhaled or exhaled.

The plan had apparently worked, for the Dragon was distracted by his own breathing. Now was the time for Sword Cross Chance to play the hero, to save the day, to sink the Titanic.

He lifted up the harpoon and lunged at the Ice Dragon. The Creature was so perplexed by the sound of his own breath that it did not notice the advancing hero or his sinister weapon. Sticking home, Sword Cross Chance cleaved the creature in two equal halves. By the time the Dragon had realized what was happening, he was dead and sinking to the bottom of the ocean blue.

A roar of applause filled the air as Sword Cross Chance gave a well-earned bow to his adoring fans. Mace Righteous and Romeo Red clapped loudly and stomped their feet on the deck of *The Unsinkable Molly Brown*. Christopher Havok, from the observation deck of Romeo's flying craft, just stared mutely at the scene and then bit his lip.

"Well done," cried Romeo Red.

"My hero," gushed Mace Righteous.

"It would seem that all of my hard work has paid off once again," Sword Cross Chance said as he jumped to the deck of the ship landing beside his friends. "However..."

"However what?" said Mace. "It was perfect!"

"Well there were a few finer points that ran afoul of my studies. I would not expect a novice to history such as yourself, to have noticed these things my lovely Mace Righteous. Next time, I will get it right. Places everyone!" The entire battle scene reversed itself to the start. The Titanic arose from the deep and reformed, the Pirates jumped back into place with only a few of them complaining about having to be slaughtered again. Sword Cross Chance smoothed out his outfit and was prepared to start again.

"Well, as much as I enjoyed your re-enactment Sword. I have my own work to attend to," said Romeo Red as he headed back to his own aircraft.

Mace Righteous called out to him, "Give my regards to that bad boy Neon Mercy when you see him next."

"Should I happen upon him again, I will certainly do so my dear," but he, like myself, has many complex responsibilities to the cosmos and such."

Sword Cross Chance waved goodbye to his friend as the gangplank was pulled back and Romeo's beached bleached whale took its leave.

"He works too hard," Mace Righteous said to Sword Cross Chance. "I wonder what he finds so fascinating about Ert anyways?"

"Earth," Sword Cross Chance corrected. "Now..... Action"

And the battle began again.

The End Again

Tale of the Seventh Sign
By Randy A. Cook

Of Sight and Hidden Knowledge
Tale of the Seventh Sign
Chapter One

Of mighty stones, the walls were made. Torches pushed back the dark. In a realm dreamed of by some and dreaded by others, a God fears for his children. Ancient Asgard has watched the race of man rise and fall, and now ponders its rise again.

A fortress chamber high in a tower, a God considers his people's tomorrow, Lord High Father, Master of Gods, the keeper of a coming sorrow.

The skins of lions, tigers and bears covers the floor upon which a broad armored form passed back and forth before an archway. Through the arch, a balcony of cut stone and mason. At long last, the form stopped, and then moved out onto the balcony. Brow drawn tight and eyes intense, the being scanned the field of stars that lay before him.

An hour passed and then another.

The God lifted his gauntleted hands into the air, palms open, fingers wide. Words of thunder broke from his lips:

"Where be thee damned prophet of our death?! Where starts the Ragnarok?"

Iron gauntlets formed fists and with fury, he smashed at the cold, coarse stones of the railing.

"All seeing, All knowing, I Odin command this revelation…" He waited, expecting an answer, but no answer came. Odin walked slowly, pondering what

71

he could not see, back into his chamber and sat himself on a great granite throne.

Two ravens of jet black swooped down from the sky, entering through the open arch and took rest, each on a shoulder of Odin. Lord Odin listened to the winged ones silent signals and sighed, then answered the invisible voices:

"Having flown the width of the heavens thou return empty, knowing nothing more than before."

Grasping for an answer, the Master of Gods, sat in contemplation. He reached and tugged once at a braided rope hanging to his left. In the distance, a great bell rang clear. He reached to his right and took hold of a carved ivory pipe. As he finished packing it with the leaves of some mountain herb, a Valkyrie timid, eyes low, advanced to his feet.

"A brand," Odin said.

The maiden immediately took an ember stick and lit her master's pipe.

The Lord of Asgard breathed deep of the aroma then said, "Fetch me my High-seer, fetch me Ezkanta."

Counsel is Sought
Tale of the Seventh Sign
Chapter Two

Ezkanta having entered the chamber, paid homage unto Odin and addressed his Lord's troubles:

"Hail Odin, All Father of Gods. I have been summoned and made hast to thine call. My voice echoes thy own. When the God Blader was slain, his pyre fulfilled the sixth sign. I too have wondered at the beginning of the end, my Lord. I spoke of such with your son Thor earlier this very eve, until weary sleep called him to his slumber. He rests in his chambers below these thy very own."

Ezkanta stood near the balcony arch, his robes moving in the breeze. He looked toward Odin and continued:

"In time, before time had meaning, the three fates foretold, the seven signs of Ragnarok unfold. All Asgard suspects, but only thou doest truly know."

"For I have been witness to six of the seven! And now I seek for the final and fatal. It is near of this I fear," Odin drew breath, "Know my dilemma Ezkanta, I, All seeing father of the Gods, have sought a glimpse and gathered not. To the farthest ends, from Bifrost to Midgard and all between. All seeing I may be, alas, all knowing I apparently am not. What tiny corner have I not sought? Where be Ragnarok?"

Ezkanta lowered his head and replied, "You honor me my Lord. If thou doest know not, then surely it has not come to pass."

Odin challenged, "You have sight beyond sight seer. Where do you look?"

Head low and tilted, eyes peering from the side, a questioning glance then Ezkanta replied:

"I have seen a future, all dark and dead, Asgard to the scavengers might be feed. Choose carefully great Lord, what you ask and seek or thou will rule a kingdom of rotting meat."

"I care not for thy riddles seer. My sword may grow thirsty unraveling thy words. If you know not where I am to look, then reveal unto me he who does. This, I am sure you hide!" Odin's eyes flashed with a warrior's rage.

Ezkanta bowed and answered, "By sooth I speak as thou hast commanded. No God can answer and hold it just, but rather a force not felt since creation. A dragon of creation… and perhaps the beast of destruction."

Odin smiled at this and said to continue. And Ezkanta did:

"From the chaos fires the worlds were formed both that of Gods and that of men. With solidification of pure power, all matter and life were made. Partial order imposed on chaos. Therefore, within all things born of the creation fire, the fire still lingers within. Petition the fire, and thou petition all things."

Odin asked, "How do I summons this Creation Fire, and ask what must be asked?"

Ezkanta answered, "A place must be made to withstand the pain, but of no common substance must this be done, for none can stand before pure chaos and retain a form of order. From the heart of the sun, a metal of True Gold is found. Of this must be fashioned a brazier within which the fire may burn, that the Dragon may manifest. I have incantations said to call forth a well of knowing fire into this place, and then may you command your queries be answered. If knowledge of the place of the seventh sign is to be gained, then you must petition that spark which exist in all places created to explain."

Odin stood, "Then as thou have said, let it be done. I instruct Hugin and Munin to take wing and fly to this heart of the sun and retrieve a Gold that is True."

From their master's shoulders the black ravens took flight, on strong wings they were up and gone, as their Lord commanded.

To Wake the Great Dragon Pyro
Tale of the Seventh Sign
Chapter Three

And under the direction of Ezkanta, a brazier was built of True Gold from the sun, brought to Asgard by Odin's Ravens of Jet. And Odin placed his Runes upon a seal around the urn that it might constrain chaos from taking all Asgard unto itself.

In the center of the chamber between the balcony archway and the great granite throne, the brazier was set firm on the floor. It measured three times a man's length in diameter and rose to the waist in height. On its golden surface were the symbols of power that Ezkanta required. And etched on the stone floor in a circle around the brazier, Odin placed his Seal and marks on his command.

When all manner of preparations had been completed, Odin barred all save himself and Ezkanta from his chamber and ordered that none should enter. He also ordered two valkyries of silver shield and helm to stand watch and guard the hall before his door that none might venture passed. Ezkanta then vanquished all light from the room, and only twilight shone in from the sky outside the balcony archway.

Odin set himself upon his throne and watched, a great shadow among shadows.

Ezkanta began his incantations, ancient Words of Making, Magicks to summons the sleeping Inferno, conjuring to bore a well of knowledge. Ezkanta did set his mind in a particular pattern, and spoken on high with chant and thought.

Odin did feel a shift, a breeze began to stir. A faint murmuring of voices in the distance grew ever nearer. A multitude of whispers filled the chamber. The breeze became a wind and the wind became a gale. From all directions, words did fly as the brazier did suck all breath unto its bowl.

Odin steadied himself and gripped the arms of his chair least he be pulled towards the golden urn. Ezkanta fell to the floor and laid still, his robes fought to free themselves and fly to the center of the room.

Odin watched as a thousand screams and shouts smashed into the urn. Swirling clouds formed a funnel over the brazier. Thunder shook inside the funnel, and fierce lights flashed through the smoke. A great roar began. So deep as to push all thought asunder. A blinding curse struck into the urn and shadows were cast revealing menacing forms and shapes.

Then silence. No motion, no light.

Odin looked questioning towards the golden urn. "Have we failed?" he stood and advanced towards the urn. Odin approached until arms distance from the gold container, when an explosion rocked his stance and he gazed into the blood red flame now filling the urn.

"Who calls me from sleep? Who dares wake the Dragon of the Inferno?" the Flame spoke.

And Odin replied, "I Odin, All-Father of Gods, Master of Asgard dare."

The Flame rose even to touch the ceiling and said, "A God??? I see you have a fire within you that is your own, a self, and a soul! Does this make you a God?"

Odin drew into himself his power, "I have commanded thou to come and reveal knowledge unto me. Do not mock me or I shall extinguish thine heat."

Odin's power swelled and revealed itself in light and heat equal to that of the fire elemental's. And Odin said:

"Your power is spent in a creation; you have not the energy to waste by vast displays of might."

"Indeed you are wise Odin. I am nearly spent, but know this, I am still mighty and not to be trifled with."

"Agreed, we understand one another," Odin said grimly.

The Flame: "What would you have of me? Be quick, I wish only to slumber until I may take back what I have given, till the next cycle."

Odin answered: "You are in all things created, thus you must know what transpires in all things. Tell me where the final and fatal sign to show the coming of Ragnarok is?"

The Flame replied, "You understand not the truth of creation. Indeed, I am in all things created and in part, in all things to be created. But I am finite; else, I would overcome and destroy you, then return to my slumber. I am not All seeing, but…"

"But what? Speak Flame or be extinguished"

"Only a great God is All seeing, but a God does not know where to look. I, as creator could find the place, but am not All seeing and cannot look. If I were All seeing I would spy and then show you."

"Then all is lost, and doom shall take us in our ignorance." Odin's hopes fell; he turned his back on the Flame and stared out the archway looking blindly once again at the field of stars.

"Wait little God, I have a bargain to offer you."

Odin said over his shoulder, "You have nothing to barter with if you cannot show me the sign."

"But I will show you. If you are willing to pay a price that will allow me to see the sign hidden from you."

Odin turned and faced the Flame, "What is the price and I will pay it."

"Make me that which is All seeing… give me your sight Odin… give me your eye," the Flame sparked.

Odin Ponders His Decisions
Tale of the Seventh Sign
Chapter Four

Odin laid the body of Ezkanta on a bed next to his son Loki.

"I watch you slumber my young son, and wonder what will become of you should Ragnarok arrive. Ezkanta has told me in times past that he has seen a great darkness fall about thee, a darkness that clouds his future sight. Is this Ragnarok, he sees taking you? You have not even reached your manhood."

Odin paced beside the bed of young Loki. As he walked, a glint caught his eye. He reached down and picked up that which was hidden part by illusion and part by concealment; he shattered the illusion, and cast aside its cover to reveal a jeweled apple.

Odin looked at the sleeping Loki, "Thou art a clever godling my son, to pilfer a ruby fruit from the gardens of Freyr, and have no scars to betray your thieving. Freyr guards his gardens well and frowns most stoutly on those who trespass them. I shall have to remember to punish you for this on the morn."

Through the door, Odin walked, and Loki opened his eyes and sighed a nervous sigh.

Into the chamber of his eldest son, Thor, did Odin next wander.

"I worry for you my son, what a shame if Ragnarok were to come now while you dream. We all must die, but to die by any other way than a blade is a great sorrow. What am I to do?"

Odin brushed his hand through the blond hair of his sleeping son.

"Nay, such a death shall not befall you. I shall see to this, no matter the cost. I will pay it."

The Price is Paid
Tale of the Seventh Sign
Chapter Five

"You have an answer great God Odin?" said the Flame moving slowly to and fro in its golden urn.

"You knew what my answer would be Flame, you know I need the time and place of the seventh sign," Odin said, "it is but one more scar to celebrate my battles."

Odin dug the fingers of his sinister hand into his face. Not a sound did he utter as he plucked forth his eye and tossed it into the blood red Flame.

A massive roar escaped from the Flame as it consumed the All seeing eye of Odin. An array of images filled the fire and flashed across the blood red tongues of burning vapors. The flames stretched out like great wings of orange, yellow and red as the mouth of the Dragon fire opened wide, then closed in an ever so slight smile.

"My answer cursed Flame. Where is the time and place of the seventh sign?"

The Flame grew still and quiet, then it whispered, "I require till dawn to search out your desires my Lord Odin. Sit yourself upon your stony couch and wait."

Ragnarok Revealed
Tale of the Seventh Sign
Chapter Six

Odin watched the Flame with growing suspicion. It was almost frozen in time and space. Unmoving, like a fly in amber. The Lord of Asgard tapped his metal clad fingers against the stone armrest of his throne. Then he said in a low deep voice more to himself than to the Flame:

"You had best search well. I will have my answers. Ragnarok will not take Thor or Loki or Hiemdall, or any other God while I lead my people. Not while I can still command my powers. Nay it shall not pass till I have passed, and my mind given over to infinity."

Odin reached for his carved ivory pipe and his pouch of herbs. He packed his pipe, rose, and walked to the side of the living Fire, the Dragon of Creation. "Thou shall serve me Flame, with answers and deeds." Odin laughed and lit his pipe from the sentient Flame, "a mighty Dragon or a matchstick?"

The potent Odin drew a deep breath and walked out onto the balcony and stared at the stars, "Dawn will come soon and I will have my answers." Odin stared down upon Midgard and watched the race of man play until the morning star was nearly to shine over the twin peaks of Asgard.

"You are coming back now my Flame, I can feel it." Odin emptied his pipe of its smoldering embers over the balcony railing.

A crackle came from behind him, and Odin spun. The Flame moved freely now growing in size, increasing in heat, radiating with light.

Odin returned to his granite throne, watched the Flame stretch, and flex its fiery muscles.

"You still wait mighty Odin?" the Flame purred.

Odin: "I will surely douse thy spark if you betray me. I have paid your price; I have given you my eye, my all-seeing sight. Now give me the answer. What and where is the seventh sign of Ragnarok?"

"Fear not little God, by sooth, you have paid my price, sated my hunger, and a tasty morsel at that. I will show you the sign and the deed, not because you might destroy me, but rather, because it amuses me."

The Flame began to swirl, a whirlwind of fire. Waves of heat and brilliance spun in tight circumference. A mighty tornado from brazier to ceiling swaying and swinging in rhythm to a silent and violent song. The pinnacle of the fire fury began to bend low, and Odin found himself staring into the eyes of the storm.

Odin witnessed:

The jewels of Asgard show bright on the towers. The golden walls and arches of Valhalla glittered in the warm glow of the sun. Odin smiled as he watched Asgard at its height.

Then a shadow fell upon a tower, then another, across the golden walls of Valhalla, and blackened even Bifrost's bright lights. Odin's gaze rose up to seek out what would cause such a monstrous shadow. He peered high into the sky to see what thing could possibly be so large as to blot out the blazing sun.

Eye to eye, Odin meets with a gaze, a Cyclops of black iron and steel, feet on the ground and head in the heavens. A gasp escaped Odin's now dry mouth, as he watched a familiar metal clad fist smash down the walls of Valhalla, another crushed the high tower of Odin, and a steel clad boot shattered the Bifrost bridge.

Odin's eye, and a bloody socket, grew wide and rolled up into his head. A curse spewed forth from the God's mouth, "May you burn in hellfire for this Dragon."

"I am hellfire, my Odin," the Flame laughed.

To his knees fell the Lord of Asgard.

Small Wonders
Tale of the Seventh Sign
Chapter Seven

Behind a pillar and high on the wall, from a secret place known not by all, two small eyes watched and wondered what was in a flame to make his father fall.

Loki waited and saw his father Odin rise shaking from the floor. He watched in morbid fascination as his sire stumbled to the door. He saw his father take effort to stand straight, and open the wooden chamber gate. Only when the oak door had been closed, did Loki climb down from his spying pose.

The voice of Odin could be heard from the hall:

"Bar this door that none shall tread its threshold again! Let no noble God of Asgard enter and witness my sin. Or death most surly he will win."

The young God now focused his attention on the Flame. With small curious steps, Loki circled the brazier.

"Hello Loki most favored of the Gods. I have been waiting for you, come closer and feel my warmth... yes, that's right... I have much to teach you."

-So ends the Tale of the Seventh Sign-

Falling Dragons
By Randy A. Cook

Planet Fall
Falling Dragons
Chapter One

A small electrical spark was followed by a fiery burst of light and heat. A violent crack of thunder shook the command cabin... a sound that would never escape the hull of the starcraft. The brilliance and fire of the explosion were sucked away moments after creation by an immense void contained within a tiny speck of nothing. A puncture wound in space opens, for a fraction of a second, and then heals itself. The starship that collided with this tiny black hole however does not heal. Time and space is resilient, the works of men are not quite so durable.

"System, online, give me a report of the damage in the warp fields." The voice was calm despite the screaming siren that filled the small cabin of the starship DragonFly.

A cold voice replied.

SYSTEM: "27% maximum potential in field space fold; time distortion negligible; 76% maximum potential in ranged spatial drive."

"Blast! Not enough warp field left for a fold into a space lane... System, scan for the nearest hospitable planet that we could reach before the life-support and drive engines give out."

A bank of lights on several hard drives began oscillating as the computer searched its databases. 17 seconds later the cold voice replied.

SYSTEM: "Scan completed. Limited data available indicates suitable planet bearing: 46.8-Y, 12.798-X, 87.00123-Z. Range 2897u"

Another explosion near the back of the ship rocked the young pilot forward, forcing him to grab the control deck in an attempt to maintain his balance. The ship's computer responded.

SYSTEM: "23% maximum potential in field space fold; time distortion negligible; 69% maximum potential in ranged spatial drive."

"At least time is still constant. I won't have to die before I was born." The young man laughed as he sat down in his high backed command chair.

"System, enter coordinates into guidance and lock down what's left of the ship." A cough escaped from his mouth; smoke had begun to fill the tiny chamber. "And start sending a distress signal." A low vibration shook the ship. This in itself was a sign of trouble, since normal course adjustments and movements in space generally caused no indications detectible by humans. The acceleration could be felt as the guidance computers took hold and directed the flight.

SYSTEM: "Life support failure in 16.4 minutes; estimated time of arrival to target planet in 14.8 minutes."

"A little close, but I can't be choosy." Pushing a lock of dark brown hair from his eyes, the pilot of the stricken ship examined the video monitor on the dash to the left of his command chair.

"Give me all your planetary data on the target."

Text and graphics began to scroll across the monitor's video screen. With an authority of calm, the young man read the material as it was flashed across the screen.

Target name: Sigma D-1, 3rd planet of the twin stars of D'17 and D'18. A system with two yellow G type stars. D'18 follows a tight orbit around the lead star D'17. Sigma D-1 orbits D'17 with an average distance of 159,483km. Planetary Atmosphere: Acceptable to sustain humanoid life. Gravity: 1.2 normal. Other: Vegetation and animal life present. Sustained complex biosystem. (Galactic survey 145.49.2 indicates numerous plants toxic to non-indigenous life forms) Dominate life form: Mammal, humanoid, Civ rating level 3.2; no further data available.

"I didn't plan on staying long enough to sample the local delicacies anyways." The pilot smiled a weak smile. "System, define Civ rating 3.2. Are the natives going to add me to their lunch menu or am I poisonous to them as well?"

SYSTEM: "Civ rating level 3.2 defined as: verbal language present, tribal style culture, hunter\gather culture, fire present, early standard earth\sky religious concept present. This rating gives no indication of cannibalism."

"OK, that's a relief. I would have preferred to leave a bad taste in their mouth though. Would serve them right if they did decide to eat me," the young man said as he reached out and patted the cabinet that contained the main AI processors for the ship's Interactive Control System.

The digital readout on the main control panel indicated just under six minutes until arrival.

The young man strapped the restraining belts over his chest and across his waist; next he pulled the padded crash bars down from the top of the chair and secured them into place around his body. Although the bars and restraints were designed to hold the occupant in place during the controlled, but rapid acceleration and deceleration of take offs and landings from a gravitation body, they should serve well by preventing him from being tossed around during a not so controlled emergency landing. The flight manuals preferred to avoid the word, "crash".

System: "Outer hull temperature increasing to 146 degrees. Atmospheric penetration beginning." A metal heat shield slid down covering the observation portal, but not before the pilot caught a glimpse of the planet he was about to hit at a probably fatal speed, or before he saw the reflection of the sparks that were consuming his guidance computers.

System: "Optimum emergency landing location identified and entered into guidance comput…"

The air was fresh, so unlike the recycled version that was the hallmark of space flight. The rise and fall of Gregory Emerson's chest quickened a bit. Consciousness came slowly and painfully.

"Ohh my head… hey! I'm alive. Damn! I really am alive." He looked about the cabin. The emergency lighting showed the charred and twisted computer controls, several support beams had buckled and numerous floor and ceiling panels had torn free and laid scattered about the room.

Gregory unlocked the belts and released the "crash" bars from their safety position. He rose from his chair, only to fall to his knees on the metal surface of the floor. Hands and teeth clenched tightly as a blaze of fire passed through his side. The pain ran up and down the length of his chest.

"Feels like I might have broken a few ribs. Guess I'm pretty lucky, it could have been worse," he looked around the room at the wreaked controls, the gaping holes in the hull, and the blood on the tunic of his flight suit. "Yeah... Pretty lucky. Right System?"

"System???..." Gregory waited a moment.

"System are you still with me?" Gregory's eyes narrowed as he looked towards the System's main cabinet.

A crackle escaped from the speaker, then a low hiss. After a few moments..."

System: " 34% maximum potential in AI system. Re-routing energy reserves."

"Good, I thought I might have lost you." The young man propped himself up against a fallen girder beam. "Report ship's damage."

System: "Outer and inner hull breached in 7 locations, 4 critical, 3 minor; guidance computers inoperable; life support inoperable; 6% warp energy remaining; field space fold inoperable; ranged spatial drive inoperable; long ranged communications inoperable; short ranged communication inopera..."

"Stop!!" Greg cut the mechanical voice off. "I understand already." A frown of intense thought lowered itself over the wounded pilot's face. "Did you get a distress signal out before everything went inoperable?"

System: "Access to outgoing communications Log files inoperable."

He reached out and grabbed a metal railing that had come loose in the landing. If indeed you could call it a landing. Skipping across an unknown planet's atmosphere like a stone on a lake. Then scraping the planet's surface to slow and finally halt your plunge is not what Greg could or would call a true landing. But he was alive and in need of a crutch. He had to use what was on hand, and a fallen metal railing would do just fine. He thought he would have to do a lot more improvising in the very near future if he was going to make it until help arrived, assuming that the distress call made it out.

Grasping it tightly, he made his way to one of the holes in the hull and examined it. The inner and outer hulls were ripped completely though with several power conduits severed with sections missing, obviously sucked out through the hole. The emitters for the structural reinforcement fields hung swinging in the gap. The hole was large enough for Greg to not only see the outside world, but also big enough for him to step through.

The DragonFly had come down blind on the dark side of the planet. "A bloody miracle," Greg thought to himself. The ship's outer floodlights illuminated a large area of the night, but it was still difficult to make out the edges of the clearing that the ship had crashed upon. Exhaust vapors permeated the area outside from his degenerating warp field. He saw only the vague outline of trees, rocks and debris from the relative safety of his ship's interior.

Since nightfall concealed the outside, Greg continued to examine the hole itself. He reached up to the top of the wall where the main crack in the ship's hulls began. As he stretched to finger the peak of the opening, the pain in his side flared. A flash of red filled his vision, and pain pushed conscious thought from his mind. He slumped and slid down the wall onto the floor, unconscious.

His pain induced blackout turned into much needed sleep at some point in the night. But sleep was not peaceful, nor extremely restful. It was full of shifting dreams about fire and explosions, followed by darkness and strange menacing creatures that lurked just out of sight, waiting for the right moment to strike and devour him. His dream self stared out into the dark, and he saw yellow eyes staring back at him. He could not run, or speak, or move in any way. He could only watch, as the yellow eyes grew closer and larger. Greg could feel the pounding of his heart, as if it were trying to smash its way out of his damaged chest. And the yellow eyes just stared down upon him. The long night passed and Greg awoke bathed in light.

A forgotten kind of light not seen for many months by the young pilot. It cascaded through the rips in the hull of the twisted starship. The light of a natural sun, not LED, not fluorescent, not incandescent, but natural, clean, real solar energy. Even when he was home, the only sunlight he really experienced was through the heavy shielded glass windows of the huge orbital space habitat he called homeworld. Rarely did he step foot on Native Earth, and when he did, the gray haze and ash that permeated the upper atmosphere prevented much of the sun's energy from reaching the planet's surface. The Trial-By-Fire wars had left much of Native Earth a desolate land used primarily as a waste disposal site.

Greg raised himself up off the floor to look at the twin suns shining before him, and at the world he now beheld. It terrified him; it seemed so large and threatened to take his breath away. The well defined boundaries of the DragonFly or even the Homeworld's orbital habitats held a contained comfort that always allowed for breath, sure and steady. That was gone replaced by... this.

The vegetation was various shades of green; flowers of a pale pink dotted the view. Trees surrounded the grassy clearing where the ship had some to rest, or maybe to die would be a more accurate description. The sky was a brilliant fiery orange. The two suns, a pair of vibrant yellow orbs, had just cleared the horizon of daybreak in what Greg guessed to be the North. Planetary directions can be so confusing to a space navigator that had spent the majority of his time in the void of space.

"Looks friendly enough in the daylight", he tried to convince himself, "System, are you still here?"

SYSTEM: "Yes"

"Good, scan for life forms, particularly humanoid."

SYSTEM: "Limited scanning capacity available due to…"

"Do the best you can," Gregory said with a marked tone of irritation that was meant more for himself than the computer since he knew it could not understand something like human frustration.

SYSTEM: "Scan completed; 614 smaller life forms, probably of animal type. No obvious larger\higher life forms within one Kilometer, extended scan indicates cluster of possibly higher life forms detected 14.7 kilometers, 13 degrees West Standard."

"Just maybe, I can get some help." Holding his side, Gregory limped over to a wall panel and tried to open it. The cabinet partially opened. The frame must be slightly ajar, preventing it from sliding freely. Greg pounded on the side and knocked it free so that it fully opened. He removed a small vial, a hypodermic, some disinfectant and a large amount of binding gauze for his side. With great care, he began the painful task of removing his shirt. Fifteen minutes later, he primed the hypo with the contents of the small vial and injected it into himself. Next, he took the disinfectant spray in hand. The prophylactic medicine caused a burning sensation as he sprayed it upon the many cuts and abrasions covering his body. The most painful was yet to come; he still had to wrap his side with the bandage material. Each swathe of the dressing had to be pulled tight, and each pull brought fresh waves of constricting fire. He had to stop several times to catch his breath, but ultimately, agonizingly, succeeded. With the task complete, the painkiller was beginning to take hold and the burning ache started to subside. In hindsight, Greg thought he should have waited until the narcotic had started to work before he bound his side. Live and learn, the emphasis being live.

He closed his eyes and thought about his choices. With a shrug, he said in the direction of the computer, "I think I'll explore a bit before I try to salvage the ship. Do a diagnostic test on the surviving circuits while I'm gone."

SYSTEM: "Acknowledged. Beginning Diagnostics."

Greg went to another wall panel and pressed his hand on an imprint screen. "Open weapons' security chamber."

SYSTEM: "Verbal Entry code required for biometric confirmation."

"241-55-8321." Greg replied.

An armored panel in the wall slid open revealing a vault like drawer. The weapons' drawer was heavily reinforced so it escaped the problem of a slightly twisted frame. The design of this, as opposed to the medical cabinet, showed the priorities of the engineers who constructed it. Opening the drawer, Greg looked down at the collection of weapons it contained. Reaching in and lifting a handgun, he examined the charge level, and then strapped the holstered gun to his waist. Next, he removed a vibro blade and again checked the power level. "Good, both of these are fully charged." Greg rarely had need to open this drawer let alone take or use the items contained.

"Do what you can to start repairs, I'll be back shortly." Gregory then eased himself through a hole in the hull and into the warm, green world of Alpha D-1, under the twin suns of D'17 and 18. He heard the computer reply.

SYSTEM: "Acknowledged. Maintenance mode initiated."

The ground was firm under Gregory's boots. A light carpet of grass covered the clearing, except for the half a kilometer of plowed earth where the ship had skidded to a stop. He surveyed the area around, "so much green. I hate green."

Turning his attention back to the DragonFly, the young man shook his head as he walked around his ship, "and I just had her painted."

Omen of the Great Spirit
Falling Dragons
Chapter Two

The old man pulled the whetstone slowly over the tip of the arrow. When the edge was sharp and smooth, he set it on the wooden bench beside his bearskin mat. His gaze moved around the fire, looking into the watching eyes of the many children who waited.

At long last he spoke, but only after letting the anticipation build in the minds of the children, and he said, "Behold my children, as it was spoken to me by my father, and to him by his father, and so forth, back to the time of the great journey that brought our people to this promised land of plenty. A night, very much like this one, long ago when I was as small as many of you, my father told me what the Great Spirit said. And now, I shall tell you, "Go forth into a land where the hunt is good. I shall watch and be close, and always see what cannot be seen. The invisible, I shall give you and show you. This great knowledge shall be cast from the sky by the Gods in a time when your people are ready. The earth will shake, the sky will burn with fire, and a great noise will awaken your soul. A True Knowledge will fall to your feet. You may have this learning. Live life well, but always beware. In this time, the good and the evil of Gods shall smite one another in the heavens and you will know this by the flash of storms and the roar of thunder. The Dragon, who is the great trickster, will reach with fire into the heavens and strike at the Great Spirit... and then at man. Know that I defend you, but you must be my arrow, my spear, my chosen people. Know that the learning I shall send is meant for you, and your children, and your children's children. Receive righteousness and give justice. Use my knowledge for righteous justice. Again, I remind you of the dark one. He is the Dragon, and a cunning one who would stop man from gaining the knowledge to see beyond his smoke and spell. Go now into this land of promise. Build your fires hot and bright. Teach your children to hunt and fish. Tell them to look into the heavens and watch for the sign of the gifted knowledge."

The children's eyes were wide and full of wonder.

"When will the sign come, Wise One?" A small boy asked.

"Soon," the Old Man smiled.

"How do you know this Wise One?" asked the boy.

"Because my father's father's father told us so," he replied to the child then added, "Now to your beds little warriors, before the night grows cold and the Dragon rides the wind to find you awake and carries you off to his dessert."

The children jumped quickly and scattered out from the Old Man and his firelight to find their warm tents and waiting mothers. All save one who looked at the Old Wise Man and asked, "But how soon?"

"Very soon, for with young warriors like you T'Sal, we will be ready to defend this knowledge from the Dragon, who would steal it back." This was the Wise One's reply and this satisfied the boy for the moment, who wandered toward home and his bed.

The Old Man gathered up his arrows and skins; content to pass on his learning to the young, and so continue the Great Spirit's teachings. He then went to his own tent to sleep a contented sleep.

The night air gained a chill, the ground a coat of moisture. A thousand ancient stars filled the sky to make old and familiar patterns. A little boy unable to sleep, climbed an outcrop of rocks not far from his parent's tent, to look out into the heavens and wait for the sign of the coming knowledge. For T'Sal knew that he was ready to learn its secrets.

Long into the night, the small child's eyes grew heavy and closed. His mind grew light and he dreamed of himself wearing a headband of grand and colorful feathers. Before a great fire he sat, surrounded by many curious eyes all waiting for him to speak and tell them the story of the falling knowledge. He told them the story as he had heard it from the Old Wise Man. But as he spoke to these dream children of the falling fire, he awoke, startled by a distant sound. He glanced around feeling foolish, hoping that none had seen him jump. Then he once again looked up into the sky and gasped at what he saw.

An arc of fire crossed the sky and hit the horizon.

"Surely this is the sign the Old Wise One spoke of," the young boy thought, "And only I am awake to see it. I have been chosen to be the deliverer of God's learning to my people."

He wondered if he should wake his parents and tell them of the great sign. "No," he thought, if the Old Gods wanted them to see, they would be awake instead of me. "I will go and see God's gift and learn all that he has sent, then come back and tell my tribe. So they can learn it also."

He jumped down from his perch of stone and added, "and if this is just a dream I will not look a fool by telling them."

T"Sal ran off into the darkness of the night and left his tribe's tents and warm fires to find the fallen learning of the Gods.

The Gift of Gods &Tricks of the Dragon
Falling Dragons
Chapter Three

Gregory Emerson sat on a rock and glared at his crippled starship. He then looked out towards the forest that surrounded the clearing.

"Might as well take a look around," he thought. "I've nothing to lose."

He walked into the dense forest, and carefully studied one of the taller trees. He did not recognize the species. Botany had never held his interest. Its leaves were long and narrow, with veins of brown crisscrossing a light virescent surface. The bark was coarse, offering many handholds. He could have climbed it with ease, if it had not been for the trouble in his side. Perhaps it was a way of denying the hopelessness of his situation, but climb the tree he did. Inch by tortured inch he conquered the obstacle. From his high vantage point, he hoped he would see something, anything that might help him get off this isolated little planet.

The view from the tree top was staggering. The vastness of the landscape made him dizzy and long for the confines of the DragonFly.

The D'17 star system was located far from any of the major space lanes. This reduced the odds of a chance rescue to near nil. Not expecting much, he was not disappointed by the lack of any sign of civilization. He did however, see a small stream flowing nearby, and felt himself suddenly parched.

He carefully climbed down. Going up had been much easier than coming down, Looking below he became intimately aware of the distance between himself and hard ground so very far away. With much relief and his feet firmly on the earth he made his way to the stream.

He pulled a small device from a vest pocket and waved it close the flowing water. After a few moments, a green light flashed on its screen. He then hovered the handheld box over a nearby shrub to which it flashed red.

"Yep, the plants are toxic, but the water seems good."

After taking a good long drink, he watched the water gently drift down a natural path, and marveled at how much he missed his home planet, even as environmentally corrupted as it was. It had been months since his last planet fall, and longer still since he had taken a moment to really look at what made a planet, any planet, special. The trees, the air, even the sunlight was actually better than the recycled varieties found onboard a tiny tin can in the middle of space. Why did it scare him so much then? Why then did he always return to the space lanes? He didn't have any answers and grew tired of the stream. He began the return trip to what was left of his ship.

Greg stepped clear of the forest and into the field with his starship. He let his eyes wander around the forest edge and then across the field towards the tin can he now called home. He saw a small humanoid figure standing before his ship. His shock quickly turned to excitement as he half walked, half ran towards the figure that he was now sure was human. It would have been a full gallop, but anything beyond a brisk walk inflamed his side and the resulting pain slowed him down.

"Hey," the pilot yelled.

The small figure turned then crouched down, his feet set wide. He was ready to run or fight, whichever was required.

"You're a boy, a real human kid. Aren't you?" Greg slowed to nearly a crawl when he saw the fear that gripped the boy. He continued slowly towards the native and then stopped in front of the boy leaving several meters between them, as much for his own safety as for concern over the boy's obvious apprehension. The small native pulled a crude, but dangerous stone knife from his leather belt, and stepped back away from the pilot. Obviously, Greg had misjudged how much space the kid would require.

"Whoaaa, now kid, calm down, I'm not going to hurt you. Where are your parents?"

The boy named T'Sal narrowed his eyes and thought, "Be this strange man the Keeper of God's Knowledge, or the Great Trickster here to deceive me with illusion and smoke. A God or Dragon in the skin of a man?" T'Sal hesitated not knowing the answer. He decided to wait, and be cautious, as his father would do. He would ask questions and then decide who this man before him was.

The native said a few wary words, taking care to be respectful. If he was the servant of the Great Spirit then such respect was due; if he was the Dragon, then best not to provoke his wrath. Greg could not understand the words, but took note of the tone.

Holding his hands out before him, palms opened upward, as he had been taught in Space Guild training to do when encountering an unknown alien, Greg said, "So you don't speak Galactic Common. Hey! That's fine. My ship," Greg pointed at the crippled starcraft, and the boy's eyes followed. Greg continued, "has a hell of a computer on board. It can translate just about anything."

Greg slowly inched passed the boy and reached his ship. The boy moved to keep a good distance between them. Greg could tell that the native was not sure what to do, and might decide to run at any time.

"System, On-line Now!" Greg said over his shoulder into the rift on his ship. He spoke as loud as he dared. The fear of frightening the boy off dominated his thoughts. He hoped the computer could hear him.

SYSTEM: "On Line"

A voice from nowhere! The boy turned and bolted at the sound of the cold unnatural words from the thing hiding within the dark bowels of the metal cave. He stopped when he reached the forest edge, turned and watched the strange man; his eyes searched for he who possessed the cold voice.

"Damn," Gregory said as he brushed his hair from his eyes and then turned towards his ship. "Are your translator programs intact?"

SYSTEM: "Yes, Translator On-line."

"Good, he might come back." And as he said this, the small native boy was creeping cautiously closer.

Greg crawled into his ship and emerged a few moments later, holding what he hoped would be a good lure for the boy, candy.

T'Sal watched as Greg tore off the cellophane wrapper and took a small bite of the chocolate bar. Greg swallowed, smiled, advanced a few steps, and placed the candy bar on the ground. The pilot backed away and waited for a child's curiosity to take hold.

Sure enough, the native boy cautiously came forward and poked at the brown bar before picking it up. After sniffing it, he took a guarded bite. He ate the chocolate and said something that Greg still could not understand.

"Did you get that System? Can you translate?"

SYSTEM: "Working... Working... Accessing Galactic Survey data for similar notations. No direct interaction with native populations, but discreet observational data available. Opening new file with collected data."

The boy looked at the ship and continued talking in short, clipped, phrases. The computer picked up the sounds and continued working.

SYSTEM: "Base compiled. Translation proceeding."

"Well?" Greg questioned.

The computer translated the boy's basic words as it continued to expand its vocabulary base, "Thank you... Sky Lord... Good Taste. Voice... Who? You Keeper of Learning Gift Spirit Great?

Greg tapped his own chest saying, "I am Gregory Emerson," he then pointed towards his ship, "the Captain of the starship DragonFly. System, can you relay that?"

The computer attempted to translate Greg's words into the boy's language.

The child responded with a string of unknown words while the computer's language database grew.

Greg told the computer, "System, continual verbal translation." He looked at the child, "What's your name kid?"

The boy's eyes widened when he heard the machine say the words in the tongue of his tribe and he quickly replied, "My name is T'Sal, Warrior of the Tribe of Brokana." The boy pounded his fist against his own chest to add emphasis to the last part of his words.

The computer translated the child's meaning and Greg chucked, just a bit, at the use of the word 'warrior'.

"Good," Greg replied. "Now, where is your tribe? Your people? Are they very near here?"

The boy looked puzzled, and Greg turned to the ship and asked, "Doesn't that translate?"

SYSTEM: "Translation relayed correctly."

T'Sal then said, "You know all things Sky Lord. You know me and my tribe." T'Sal wanted to believe that this was the Keeper. "You see and hear the wind and the water. You knew I would like the brown food. More good taste please, Sky Lord?"

Greg smiled, "More candy? Sure, why not? A warrior has to keep up his strength." He crawled through the crack in the hull and motioned for T'Sal to follow.

T'Sal twisted his mouth to say the word, "KKandee." After a few moments of indecision, the boy followed. Once within the ship, T"Sal knew that this was a blessed place, sanctified ground. With holy reverence T"Sal reached out and touched the smooth metal walls of the command cabin. He starred mesmerized by the rows of blinking lights that made up the computer banks, hard drives, and controls. He said a silent prayer of thanks to the Great Spirit for showing him these wonders, and looked up at the man who was the Keeper of this place, and he knew him to be the Keeper of God's Learning.

Greg watched the boy in satisfied humor, and then told the System to open a storage locker that revealed a horde of candy bars and other goodies that Greg was so fond of, including a bottle of a cheap whiskey. He removed two candy bars and closed the panel. He would come back later, when he was alone for the whiskey. He was sure he was going to need it.

Together, he and the boy ate the chocolate; Greg questioned the native all the while, allowing the computer's translation database to continue to grow in its ability to translate the now not so alien language.

Unfortunately, the inquisitive pilot learned very little from the boy. Most of his questions were met with the answer, "You know all things Sky Lord." The one thing that he did quickly learn from the resulting conversation was that the child T'Sal held him as some kind of messenger from the Gods.

After several failed attempts, Greg gave up on trying to convince the boy otherwise.

Once again thirsty, Greg told the computer to dispense two cans of soda. Another small panel opened in the wall and a pair of disposable aluminum cans of Pepsi rolled out and were caught by Greg. "Choice of a new generation" he mused.

Gregory found himself enjoying the company of the boy. This surprised him a great deal, for he was by his nature, a solitary man and often found it difficult to be around other people. Until now, he really could not tolerate children for any length of time. Even his sister's boys got on his nerves when he would briefly visit them on the habitat rings assigned to families. He had been alone in space for a long time and did not even realize just how lonely he really was. The ship's computer had been his only companion for months on end. He often talked to it. Almost believing that it understood more than just the dictionary meaning of his words, but that illusion never lasted for long. Try telling a joke to a computer, or pulling a bluff on it in a hand of poker. It could play chess and various other games, or plot a course through a meteor cluster with perfect precision, but it lacked a sense of spontaneity, the absurd reality of a thinking mind's natural humor, with all of its successes and failures. It was not human, and did not give, or take, or feel anything more than it was programmed to do. The boy obviously held great reverence and even respect for Gregory that the Captain of this tiny little long haul freighter found flattering; he needed that feeling, even if he had yet to earn it.

SYSTEM: "Warning! Imminent Engine Phase Field Collapse. Automatic pressure release inoperable. Require manual control to correct, or implosion will occur in 1.3 minutes."

Greg jumped up and ran to the control panel where he began flipping a number of switches and checking several read-outs.

T'Sal could not understand the nature of the words, but he did understand that the Voice had given a warning and demanded that Greg respond. T'Sal saw how nervous the strange Keeper of Learning had become, and the near panic in his actions. Was the Great Spirit angry?

A roar came from the outside of the ship as the captain succeeded in overriding the automated controls. The release valves opened and vented the tremendous force that had built up in the bowels of the ship. Great clouds of smoke and steam spouted into the air for several hundred meters. As the Phase Field degenerated, it caused a static build up in the atmosphere over the starcraft. The resulting electrical discharge let loose a volley of chain lightning that flashed through the clouds. Cracks of thunder shook the ship and its occupants.

T'Sal saw the storm through the rips in the ship's hull, and hid behind an overturned table. He was frightened that his God might destroy him for some unknown wrong he had committed. A disturbing thought then occurred to T'Sal, "what if it was not my sin... but rather this stranger's." T'Sal's head slowly turned towards the pilot, who was frantically making adjustments to the controls. "What if he really is the Trickster? The Dragon hiding in a human skin".

Flash of the Deceiver
Falling Dragons
Chapter Four

"T'Sal is a strong and brave boy," the Old Wise Man reassured the boy's mother. "He most likely went to hunt the Night Hare, and lost his way in the dark. It is day now, he will find us or we shall find him."

The mother lowered her head and looked at the floor of the tepee. "I hope you are right, Wise One."

The Old Wise One was about to say more about the skill the boy possessed, when a warrior rushed into the tent.

"Wise One, a great omen in the sky! Mighty storm lights flash from the earth up into the heavens!"

Both the mother and the Wise One left the tepee to go stare up at the eastern sky.

The Old Wise One's brow drew tight and his eyes stared intensely at the storm. Great clouds rose from the ground like that of a huge fire in the forest. But never has the fire and smoke of burning wood given birth to the flashes of storm lights such as these.

The Wise One quoted the legends, "And the Good and Evil of Gods will smite one another by the flash of storms and the roar of thunder. The Trickster, will reach with fire into the heavens and strike at the Great Spirit..."

The Old One held up his arms and pointed at the blazing storm clouds. He said, "Gather all warriors unto me, we shall go and do the Great Spirit's will. We will strike at the Great Liar as he strikes at the Great Spirit."

The entire tribe of Brokana moved as a single mind with a single purpose. The women carried out bows, arrows and knives from the tents placing them on the ground before the warriors who were adorning themselves with paints. Simple patterns in dull colours. Each stroke of the hand laid a different line of greens, browns, and burnt reds. The green was the colour of life and earth, the brown was the color of man, and red was the colour of the defender.

Shields were taken and weapons drawn. The warriors set out from their camp, and headed to the east, to the black clouds of the Deceiver.

The Old Wise One led the way. The thought of a fulfillment to a lifetime of faith and legends, stripped away the years and gave him a vitality long since lost in his youth.

Divine Rights
Falling Dragons
Chapter Four

"Well!" Captain Gregory Emerson laughed, as he turned to where T'Sal crouched behind a table. "You can come out now."

"Is the Great Spirit going to kill us?" asked T'Sal, afraid to hear the answer.

Greg sat himself down in his command chair, and swiveled it around to face the boy. "No, not today at least." Greg smiled at the boy's superstition. "I think I've prevented that. But I doubt if I can ever get those Phase Fields regenerated."

The boy looked blankly at the pilot, not comprehending all of what he said, but the meaning was clear; he had stopped the Great Spirit's lightning and his wrath.

"How did you do that? How did you stop the flashing of the storm lights?" T'Sal stood and looked at the table, then stepped from behind it, determined never to look at it again.

"Simple," said Greg, "I manually overrode the computer's damaged release controls and vented the pressure that was very near critical."

"OOvvrrodd," the boy echoed.

"Yeah, most of the ship is automated or voice manipulated by the Interactive Control System of the computer. I basically turned some of it off and flipped it over to manual." He raised up his hand and wiggled his fingers.

"Voice Controlled?? How?" T'Sal looked up into the eyes of the pilot, who was sitting on his techno-throne of power.

"Watch," the pilot said, "System, turn the ship's interior lighting off for 10 seconds, and then turn them back on."

SYSTEM: "Acknowledged."

The lights in the ship dimmed, then went out. The natural sunlight of D'17 faintly shown through the cracks in the ship's hull, casting dark and deep shadows of sinister proportions. In a count of ten, the lights came back on.

Quite excited the boy asked, "Can I try your magic?"

"Sure," replied Greg with an inner smile. His logic was simple, if he showed the boy how it worked, maybe T'Sal would believe that Greg was just a normal guy, a mortal and not some kind of god, and in turn answer some questions instead of giving the, "You already know that Sky Lord," answer. Greg turned his attention to the computer cabinet and said, "System, accept additional command voice on mark." Greg told the boy to speak his name into the computer's microphone at the sound of the beep."

T'Sal did this, and then looked at the strange man\lord who called himself Greg.

"Go ahead," urged Greg, "give it a try."

"System, no light, count to ten and then light again," T'Sal offered to the computer.

SYSTEM: "Acknowledged."

The lights went out for a second time; the computer voice then counted to ten, and turned the lights back on.

T'Sal let out a great laugh, "What else can I do?"

"Not a whole hell of a lot right now. I have got to try to get some of the ship's major systems running again. Else, I'll never get off this planet. Nothing personal you understand." T'Sal did not, but followed Greg anyway. Through the ship they walked, as the pilot gathered parts and tools to begin work on the communications and scanning systems.

Greg instructed the computer system to take those particular circuits off line and run a comprehensive diagnostics on those areas to assist in the repairs.

Two hours later. Greg completed his makeshift repairs on the long and short-ranged communication units. He prayed the circuits wouldn't fry when the juice was applied. He instructed the System to bring communications and scanners back on line and run a test program. He waited for the results, when the starship's computer system disengaged the test and interrupted.

SYSTEM: "67 higher life forms detected within 100 meters. Synchronized movement patterns identified. Current positioning of life forms indicate possible attempt to surround ship and prevent unseen exiting of personnel from the ship."

Spirit to Spirit
Falling Dragons
Chapter Six

Captain Gregory Emerson stood in front of his ship. The boy T'Sal stood to his right.

Greg's eyes narrowed as he watched the warrior's of Brokana move and shift amongst the forest's edge. He saw the arrows and spears that they held at the ready. He could feel the tension of these savage men, the aggression. Looking at the boy, Greg spoke to the computer, who translated the words for the boy. "What's wrong? Tell them I won't hurt them."

The boy yelled out to his people, "Fear not my people, for this is the Keeper of God's Learning. He is not here to harm us, but to help us."

The Old Wise One stepped out from the shadows of the trees. "Be wary young T'Sal. This creature is the Great Trickster who has fallen to earth on his dying dragon. Of this I am sure!"

"No Wise One. He has shown me many great wonders, and has threatened me not once." The boy defended his new companion, an angel.

The Old Wise One shook his head and said, "I have seen with my own eyes the omens. The storm lights that he did cast into the heavens, and the dark

118

clouds that obscure the suns. He is surely the evil one. He has confused you with pretty talk and grand illusions. It is just smoke and spell. The ancient prophecy has spoken of these events that he has brought down from the sky."

The computer translated what little bits and pieces that its microphones could pick up. Although Greg did not get to hear the entirety of the conversation taking place, he knew that it was not good. Slowly, and with great care he reached down and drew the pistol he still had at his waist from its holster.

The memory images of the storm that shook the ship flashed through T'Sal's mind. The great bright lightning and black clouds that Greg said he had let loose from the metal carcass he called a ship. The strange man had said he stopped them from being destroyed. How can even an angel stop the hand of God? T'Sal knows the answer. Only the hand of the Trickster could do this, and then, only for a short while.

Greg put his hand on T'Sal's shoulder and the boy visible shuddered. The pilot asked, "What's going on? Did you tell them I won't hurt them?"

T'Sal answered, "Yes... I told them."

"Then what's wrong?"

"Nothing," T'Sal said, "I... do not know..."

"You don't know what? Greg was getting confused. What did he do? What would he do? What could he do?

The Old Wise One made a hand sign to his warriors, and a volley of arrows fell less than a meter away from Greg and T'Sal's feet.

The Old Wise One shouted at Greg, "Release the child, Dark One. Set free his body as well as his mind. Then we shall settle heaven's conflict."

The computer heard the shouted words, translated, and relayed them to Greg.

"I am not a child, Wise One," T'Sal said half aloud, and half in thought.

Greg told the boy to step away from him; he knew this was turning south real fast and wanted the boy out of harm's way. He raised his pistol and fired three short burst of high intensity energy into the treetops above the heads of the warriors of Brokana.

The boy screamed as he saw the white beams of destructive power sear the tree branches off; his eyes opened wide with fear as he fell back against the ship's hull, just as the branches hit the ground. Through gasping breathe he muttered a single line from the oral history, "The Trickster will reach with fire into heaven and strike a God... then at man."

T'Sal watched the back of the demon-man Greg, and listened to the voice of the Old One as the elder leader shouted to his people. His cries to remain calm, to banish fear, to remain strong against the evil Trickster and his fire from hand. Then T'Sal heard the Wise One call his name. T'Sal closed his eyes and listened to the Wise One's instructions.

Greg turned towards the crack in the starship's hull and waited for the computer's translation of this latest exchange between the elder and the boy.

SYSTEM: (translation follows): "T'Sal, my young warrior, you must strike at this demon and destroy its mortal form before he destroys us! Your knife is sharp, as a warrior's should be. I pray to the Great Spirit that your vision is clear of his imagined smoke, and your aim is just a sharp!"

Captain Gregory Emerson never heard the complete translation, for he was dead before the second line was finished.

Several minutes passed, no motion, no life. Then slowly, from the forest shadows the Old Wise One came forth, and behind him, the many warriors of Brokana. They found the boy T'Sal, who was no longer a boy, sitting beside the fallen body of the Dragon in human hide. T'Sal held in his hand a crude stone knife covered in blood. His eyes were grey and his expression was non-existent. The man T'Sal rose to his feet and looked around into the eyes of the tribe.

The Old Wise One stretched forth his arms to accept T'Sal into a comforting embrace. But T'Sal turned his back on the old man and walked without hesitation or hindrance to the gaps in the starship Dragonfly's hull and went inside.

The Old Wise One stared through the hole and watched as the man T'Sal walked towards the center of the room; he paused only briefly when he stepped on the discarded cellophane wrapper of a candy bar. He stopped and stared down at it for a long moment before he sat himself in Gregory's chair. The Old One heard the man T'Sal say, "System, No lights. Silent count until I say otherwise."

The lights went out, and neither the Old Wise One nor any other warrior of Brokana dared enter into the darkness of T'Sal, Slayer of Dragons.

The End

Serpent in the Garden
By Randy A. Cook

He chose a knife. There was nothing particularly symbolic about the selection, although he suspected that there would be those who would obsess over that detail. He didn't like guns. They were difficult to use, loud and ironically dangerous. More likely to maim or disfigure rather than to kill. He had considered pills, but the last time all they did was make him vomit, hours of throwing up alone in the dark, making him wish he were dead but without actually delivering on the promise. So a knife it was.

He sat and stared into the night from his bedroom window on the upper story of his home. He watched the unchanging stars in the sky as they hovered over the equally unchanging landscape that was his hometown. The world with all its colour was nothing more than varying shades of black.

Memories mixed with dreams and nightmares crossed his near waking thoughts for a moment. The feathered serpent was in the garden and like even the most beautiful of fowl or flowers at night, the grand hues were bland and its coils drew tight. He could not breathe. A small child frozen in fear standing before it in an endless alley unable to move forward or to retreat from it. He blinked and the stars dimly caught his attention.

Music played beside him. He liked music, and wished he could play. Strangely enough, he could read music, something he picked up as a child when he had once taken piano lessons. The written notes stuck, but the playing just never seemed to take. Music was something special. A simple song could change your mood, lift your spirits or darken a disposition. It could bring joy or allow pain. Still, something deep inside guides the selection of the music in the moment. He felt pain and the chords either trailed the sensation or led the way. Even when we recognized the need to hear something different, upbeat, something to pull us back from the edge of... something. Some. Thing. He wouldn't do it. He knew better, but could not turn his head, lift his arm or change the station that was picked. Some Thing held him tight in a vice grip. There has to be something, some reason, some excuse. Some Thing to blame. They would want, need, something to blame. Pointing your disapproving finger at it would just make you feel better.

"If he had just been stronger, not so weak," or "he was just too hard, too strong willed and needed to be a bit softer, weaker," they might say. It was because he was black or because he was white. He was too poor or maybe too rich. He took too many meds, or he did not take enough meds, or he took the wrong meds. Grief, regret, love, lust, humiliation, pain, shame, and suffering. On and on it would go, no one even noticing that the biggest darkest secret was never revealed, never spoken, never written down. Those few and simple words that would have answered all would never be put into a single sentence with a resounding period placed at the end. That one missing sentence which would have left him completely naked, revealed to the world for all to see. We all have our secret, and we all tell our lies to hide that secret. We put on our mask, smile our polite smiles, tell our pointless stories while listening to others tell their equally pointless stories and pretend that nobody knows. Maybe they do, maybe they don't, but I am certainly not going to tell them. For some it's a small seemingly insignificant surreptitious thing, but a thing that we fear, no, a thing that we KNOW would break us into a thousand little pieces that could never be reassembled with our dignity intact. And maybe, we don't want to be glued back together anyway, stacked as we were, with fine lines for cracks reminding us of our flaws. The same flaws as before, but this time with spider web scars as constant reminders that we can never be "normal". After all, we obviously were never normal in the first place, just better liars than most. But back to the point, he laughed a sick little laugh at his choice of words. The point, hard and sharp. It's better this way.

He looked down at the stain slowly spreading out on the carpet directly below where his arm hung by his side. He had expected a rhythmic drip, drip, drip, but instead was a bit surprised by the steady stream that flowed like a faucet left open just a bit. The knife was the right choice.

###

He put the pen down and read over what he had just written. After making a few minor changes, mostly correcting grammar, he collected the papers that made up the final paragraphs and headed downstairs to get a drink. He hadn't decided yet if it would be a soda, Dr Pepper being his favorite poison of choice, or perhaps something stronger tonight.

Walking into the kitchen, she briefly looked up and asked what he was doing.

He put the stack of papers down on the table. "Putting the final touches on the ending of the book," he said getting a glass from the cupboard.

She picked up the last page and skimmed it. "It's dark, maybe the darkest thing you have ever written."

"It's an honest ending, I think," he said reaching for the Vodka. At least he had made up his mind on one thing. "I want people to understand what it's like, really understand. Maybe then they won't judge, or won't just let it go... won't let it happen."

"Sure," she said returning her attention to her phone.

He dropped a couple of cubes of ice into his drink, paused for a moment, and then opened the kitchen drawer, the one three paces left of the kitchen sink. He picked up his favorite knife. It was your basic knife, good for many things. It could thinly slice a piece of meat with ease. He put the knife quietly in his pocket.

He returned to the table were his latest work was setting and stood for a moment. Waiting, expecting, hoping and then gathered up the papers. Turning, he left the room and headed back up stairs to sit and stare out the window, and maybe listen to some music.

Sir Andrew
Or the Unfulfilled Knight

By Randy A. Cook

Through the forest green, did the young knight move. Trees towered high above him and cast long shadows over the grasses and shrubs that covered the footsteps of the massive wooden giants.

He held his sword at ready, although he knew that the timber held him no real menace. The danger was yet to come. The true test of his resolve would come not from the beast of this natural setting, but rather from the ancient creature hidden from a rational man's mind. The Dragon that dwells within the dark corners of the human soul. The worm given birth by man's perversion of God's gift. The realization that is the immortal terror within us all. Sir Andrew would face this monster soon, for deep within these walls of living lumber, at the heart of the forest, the ancient and perpetual Dragon did dwell. This was Sir Andrew's destination, a young knight's quest, his claim to fame, a reason for living and dying.

The forest was quiet and still, save for the occasional squawk of a bird, or the rustling of the leaves above by the smaller animals that scrambled there. The sound made by the foot falls of the knight were few and far between. The majority of the ground was layered with a soft, moist covering of grasses both green and fresh. If not for the breakage of a twig or the brush of a weed stock, the forest would not have noticed the passage of a mere mortal man in these timeless paths of silent timbers.

The light of the sun began to fade, and so too did the strength of the young warrior, as if the two were linked by some mystic force, the light of day and power of a man. One was the other and the other was the one. The vanity of mankind.

Against a mighty oak did he pitch his camp. He gathered fallen branches and struck a fire to hold the night at bay. A frail imitation of his precious daystar. Dried food from his provisions he prepared and ate with a hunger spawned by his day's journey. His shining shield with family crest became his pillow. Helm at his side and sword across his chest, sleep overtook this youth of baby brown curls and bright blue eyes. An oak ten times his own age was his headboard and he dreamed of his own immortality.

By the first light of Sol, the mortal man was awake and had packed his camp. He was near his goal and could not spare another moment before he would face his death and his rebirth. With great care, he did set his warrior's helm beside the old oak, between the protruding roots it was to rest.

Through the forest, he continued his journey and at long last, he found the outer lair of the immortal Dragon. It was exactly as he had expected it. In the heart of the forest, a cave stabbed deep into the earth. Sir Andrew stared into this blackened well and wondered if the Dragon would also be as expected.

A noble man Sir Andrew was born, having lived the majority of his twenty-seven years as he had been told to live. His father had planned his life. His mother helped him follow the plan, and his wife married the plan. They weren't always the same plan, for each person has their own interpretation of such things. Every person that is, except Andrew. The precise details had changed. The colours might be a bit faded in some areas or brightened in others, but Andrew took pride in this canvas, even if he had little to do with the grand composition. He thought that these minor brush marks of his own choosing were prime examples of self-will; his contribution was in the minor details if not the major brush strokes. But the master design was never altered, it was always there. Sir Andrew had just missed it. Or had he? Perhaps he had known it was there all along or had seen a flickering glimpse, but he would not, could not, look at it fully. That was about to end. There is no such thing as free will, only limited choice. And this was one choice no one would expect of him. The cave and the immortal Dragon within were his key to escape from a life that was not his own. The cage was about to be opened, and to step forth from that cage, he would need to step into the cavern before him, into an unknown, the unplanned. A new life unburdened by other's expectations. Even if that new life led to death.

From his smaller sheath, he pulled his dagger and plunged the blade into the ground near the cave entrance. Without fear, he walked into the mouth of the earth.

The natural stone walls were damp and cool. Stray beams of sunlight shifted down the tunnel from behind him, illuminating twisted drapes of granite and limestone. As he moved deeper into the earth, the light dwindled away, leaving only darkness.

From his pack, Sir Andrew withdrew a torch and tinderbox. The blaze of the fire set strange and distorted shadows dancing against the glistening rock walls. The shades of lost decisions and missed opportunities.

The trickling sound of water caused him to pause and stare down into a pool worn into the stone floor by countless millenniums of continual dripping. He looked at his own image held there and watched the reflections of his life on the water's changing surface. Each drop from the cavern's ceiling caused a slight ripple of the many memories from his past. His father had sent the face reflected there to a town not so near his family's estates for some obscure and forgotten reason. His mother had insisted that he be the one to do this for his father, and his wife had told him to collect gifts for her while he was there. He was not there. He had come here instead to create something for himself. This menial task would not be like any of the other menial tasks he had been called upon to perform, for he was not supposed to be here, or to do what he was planning to do. Into the water, he cast his shield. It sank and came to rest on the smooth bottom of the crystal clear pool. Sir Andrew could still see the family crest painted upon the metal surface as it laid motionless under countless gallons of secret water that obscured nothing, but hid everything.

Through the twisting and turning tunnels, he explored. After many hours the exploring became wandering and the wandering became rambling. He walked through the caverns with their massive towers of magnificent quartz shimmering to his left and the great mounds of bat dung piled to his right. Deeper and deeper he spiraled down into the earth.

Sweat now covered his brow, for the coolness of the damp underground had been replaced by an ever-increasing heat. Like a moth drawn to the flame, he followed the heat on its path to a world within a world. At long last he found himself in a chamber so large as to have no distinguishable ceiling, and save for the solid peninsula upon which Sir Andrew stood, the floor was a sea of churning lava. The rocks of many ancient times moved and flowed in rivers of bright red, orange, and black streaks.

Sir Andrew fell to his knees at the sight and gave tears to the molten soil in a futile attempt to cool its eternal fires. Hope was lost for he could not continue. The way before him was a searing impossibility and the path back leads only to the sorrow of his previous life that he wanted no part of.

He knelt there, eyes closed tight. He knew not what to do, so he did nothing. Such is the way of man.

But the world sometimes moves without man's direct command, as Sir Andrew was about to discover, for rising from the fires was that which he did seek, the immortal Dragon.

A distorted bulk shrouded in an amour of scales. Twin horns of bony spikes protruded from the lengthy skull. Wings of fire-forged metal flexed and lava dripped from the slanted brow as ebony eyes focused upon the little mortal man who had invaded the center of his domain and now perched before him.

The jaws with jagged brimstone teeth opened in complete silence. The fangs sparked and the flames licked across the ivory flints as the mouth lingered over the kneeling man, and then a foul heat came forth. The hot breaths had words and meanings. The sound was heavy and the meanings seemed distorted. Waves of whispers and shouts combined into one voice and the beast spoke: "I am the Ageless. I am the Eternal. I am the Dragon... Who are you?"

Feeling the words and the fire of their purpose, the young warrior, Sir Andrew, opened wide his eyes and raised his head to look at the great beast before him. He answered, "I am Andrew, Knight and noble by birth." Even now, staring into the face of the eternal, he used the vestigial remnants of a title and life that he did not want and sought to end. That is how deep the teeth of our temporal and useless constructs bit and hold on.

"What do you seek so far from your fellow man, Andrew?"

"I seek my death and my life, great Dragon. I seek your death and your life. To slay or be slain, I shall live forever by the telling of my deed."

The temperature rose as the Dragon considered the words of the mortal. Then he said, "You seek my immortality. Listen well little boy of a man. You should climb free of this cavern and return to the living, for you already have an immortal life of your own. Do not tempt its loss in foolish heroics."

"You speak of my soul?" Sir Andrew questioned. "I have already damned my soul by coming before you. There are no heroics here, I have simply decided to no longer be a brave coward. I shall gather no further gain from such things. I am, if anything, a painting of a broken soul hiding in a perfect frame."

"If you have a soul, then indeed you have an immortal life, but to speculate as to whether you are human or an abomination is pointless. You cast lots with a God who uses loaded dice. Nay then, I will not speak in hearsay of an immortal soul, but rather a more animal thing. That being the eternal cycle of your blood. Your life will continue on, as you grow old and die. Your children will grow and your grand children will grow. Then they will die and on it will go."

Sir Andrew listened to the words, considered their importance and fought in inner earnest to understand, to commit, to believe in the possibility, and lost the battle. He responded to the Dragon, "Two such sons I have sired. They are of my blood, but they are my wife's immortality, for they are of her spirit and I will never be allowed to live through them. Spiritualis successionem."

"Then you would slay me and live on in songs?" The Dragon laughed and the heat beat against Sir Andrew's face.

"I could not slay thee, Great Beast. That much is clear." Sir Andrew held his sword out before himself and dropped it into the swirling waters of metal and stone. His only remaining weapon lost to the ages as it melted to become one with ageless. He continued, "and to live in song, but still walk and wake in misery is not an immortality worth having."

The Dragon raised his head and the scaled lips formed a twisted smile, "Then you wish me to slay you, and give you the eternal sleep. The ballads of your great battle and death at the claw of the Dragon would be a continual eulogy. A noble family would not let such a heroic deed go unsung, for as you have implied, your self-inflicted cowardliness is hidden behind the veil of hopes, expectations, and lies."

"I seek my eternal rest," Sir Andrew said.

"I have eaten knights and serfs alike for many reasons, some for the mere pleasure of tasting the fear in their eyes. I see no fear in your eyes. I am the Ageless. I am the Eternal. I am the Dragon... The Great Beast. The creator of Chaos and Pain. I shall grant you your immortality. But as we both know, there are many forms of immortal life."

Waves of black light shown through the Dragon's ancient eyes and a hideous inferno burned bright behind them to fire the dark light.

The Dragon looked down upon this little man and continued, "Hear me and know this truth. On the first day of the third moon, twenty-six years from this very day, I shall rise from my molten bed and strike you down. From the sky, I will descend and take you. I grant you this immortality. You shall not know death before I rise on that date. All other mortal men wake each day never knowing if the sun they see climbing in the east is the last sunrise they shall every see. You will rise to scorn the sun, and know that on that day you cannot die for your death is already set. I give you twenty-six years of immortality. No man, no beast, no event can intervene in my degree."

Laughter shook the walls and made the land tremble as the Dragon once again sank below the sea of liquid fire and brimstone. The sounds of lost humor faded away leaving only the echoes of the pained cries of the immortal man, Sir Andrew.

The End

—— ⌒ ——

Dragon Nay-Sayer
By Randy A Cook

"I have a Dragon, there, I said it. I just put it out there for all to see. Ok, maybe not see, because apparently I am the only one who can actually see my Dragon. Ok, Ok, I know what you are thinking. Nut case. But honestly, I have a Dragon. It's been following me around since I was a kid." The young man shifted uncomfortable on the couch. "You think I'm crazy right? Everyone else does."

"We don't like to use words like 'crazy' around here," said the older man as he scribbles something down on his notepad. "I take it that you have told other people about this Dragon?"

"Yeah, sure I have. Like I said, it's been with me since I was a little kid. You don't have a large green Dragon hanging around you when you are eight years old without telling somebody. My mom, my dad, my priest, and later even a therapist that my parents made me go see, even a veterinarian once."

"So you have sought professional help with this issue before?

"Hell yes, I have sought professional help! I have a Dragon following me day in and day out. I can't turn around without him being there. And the comments, he talks all the time. Over and over, the same stories. After 20 years, I already know all of his stories. You would think that a Dragon who must be, I don't know, over a thousand years old, would have a few more interesting stories to tell. I guess it shouldn't surprise me, after all, he has done nothing but HANG AROUND ME for the last couple of decades. God, wouldn't you try to find help?"

"Good point. Has this Dragon ever told you to do something like, hurt yourself or others?" the doctor asked leaning ever so slightly forward.

"Hurt myself? You are kidding me, right? You think this is actually my subconscious trying to off myself?" the young man replied with obvious agitation in his voice. "It's a Dragon, if it wanted to physically hurt me it would just step on me or eat me or something."

"I see, so no obvious intent at self harm then. And others, has it ever told you to hurt someone else?"

"What part of it being a Dragon, do you not get? It certainly would not need me to do its dirty work if it wanted to kill someone. Besides, after you get to know him, and trust me, I know this Dragon, he is really just an oversized pussycat. And not the, 'I live in an alley and will scratch the hell out of you sorta cat'."

"Ok," the doctor said, "is the Dragon here with us now?

"Ahhh... No..." the young man said glancing nervously at the window.

The action does not go unnoticed by the Psychiatrist, "you know lying to me is not going to help your situation any? If you really want my help, you must be completely honest with me. Besides, we are on the 12th floor. There is nothing outside that window."

"It has wings."

"What?"

"The Dragon, it has wings. It can fly, so being on the 12th floor really is not a problem for him. The problem is that you want me to be honest with you. If I tell you 'yes' and that there is a 500 pound dragon floating outside your window then you are going to think I am lying to you because Dragons don't exist, and if I tell you 'no', you will also think I am lying, because I already told you that I have a Dragon following me around. So what do you want me to say?"

"I believe that you think there is a Dragon outside that window," the Doctor said trying to reassure his patient. "I have your previous medical records, so I know that there are no obvious physiological explanations for what you are experiencing. You said you talked with your Priest. What did he tell you?"

"Well at first he tried to tell me that is was perfectly normal for some children to have an imaginary friend to help them cope with a number of different stresses in life," the young man said leaning back. "But I convinced him that this was no normal situation and that he was more than just your average imaginary friend."

"He's not wrong you know," the doctor replied.

"Yeah, well, after that failed attempt he moved on to telling me that maybe this friend was really a guardian Angel."

"What did you say to that?"

"HE'S A DRAGON," the patient said with extra emphasis on all three of the words. "After a long while he started using words like 'exorcism' and 'possession'."

"How did that make you feel?"

"HE'S A DRAGON... not some devil or demon. Why can't people get that? The vet gave better advice than that guy with the collar."

"Really," the doctor said shifting ever so slightly in his chair. "What did the veterinarian say?"

"He said to flush it down the toilet. Might have worked too except I have one of those environmentally friendly, low volume, high-efficiency toilets that only uses 1.3 gallons of water per flush. It would have been fine except I tried to use a plunger to finish the job. That just pissed him off."

"Let me get this straight, you tried to flush a 500 pound Dragon down a toilet?" the doctor asked in disbelief.

"Yeah, crazy I know," the patient said with a smile.

Putting his pen down on his desk the doctor says, "Well our time is almost up for the day. I would like to see you again next week."

"That's fine doc, I have to go with a friend to another appointment anyway. Yeah, I'll see you again next week."

- - - -

141

Meanwhile somewhere else entirely...

"Ok, you are going to think that this is crazy Doc, but I have a human following me around," said the Dragon leaning awkwardly against the back of the couch.

"We don't like to use words like 'crazy' around..."

--Never the end --

About the Author

For nearly three decades, Randy A. Cook, has written books, magazine articles, manuals and games, wrapping his thoughts, work, and play in various genres including science fiction, fantasy, theology, interactive fiction and technical gibberish. He continues to write and express himself in books, software, lecturing and whatever else catches his fancy while living in the great Midwest.

Also by Randy A. Cook

Science Fiction
   The Vortex
   Metal Wars 2027
Fantasy
   Castle Darkholm
   Serpents in the Garden
Theology
   The Intimate Unknown

www.ingramcontent.com/pod-product-compliance
Lightning Source LLC
Chambersburg PA
CBHW060433130626
46555CB00005B/2337